all
the acorns
on the
forest floor

TURNER PUBLISHING COMPANY
Nashville, Tennessee
www.turnerpublishing.com

ALL THE ACORNS ON THE FOREST FLOOR

This is a work of fiction. All the characters and events portrayed in this book
are either products of the author's imagination or are used fictitiously.

Cover design: Lauren Peters-Collaer
Book design: Karen Sheets de Gracia

LIBRARY OF CONGRESS CATALOGING-IN-PUBLICATION DATA
Names: Hooper, Kim, author.
Title: All the acorns on the forest floor / Kim Hooper.
Description: Nashville, Tennessee : Turner Publishing Company, [2020] |
    Summary: "All the Acorns on the Forest Floor tells the poignant and
    moving stories of multiple characters linked by their experiences as
    mothers, daughters, and lovers. Rife with stunning imagery, masterful
    character development, and heart rendering storytelling, this book will
    captivate readers of all walks of life"—Provided by publisher.
Identifiers: LCCN 2020029256 (print) | LCCN 2020029257 (ebook) | ISBN
    9781684425297 (hardcover) | ISBN 9781684425303 (epub)
Subjects: LCSH: Domestic fiction.
Classification: LCC PS3608.O59495 A79 2020 (print) | LCC PS3608.O59495
    (ebook) | DDC 813/.6—dc23
LC record available at https://lccn.loc.gov/2020029256
LC ebook record available at https://lccn.loc.gov/2020029257

9781684425297 Hardcover
9781684425303 eBook

PRINTED IN THE UNITED STATES OF AMERICA

20 21 22 23   10 9 8 7 6 5 4 3 2 1

all the acorns on the forest floor

Kim Hooper

TURNER
PUBLISHING COMPANY

For Mya. Again and of course.
And for Chris. For everything.

contents

notes for a eulogy • 1

what we cannot know • 27

days that used to be • 53

thinking twice • 72

all the acorns on the forest floor • 87

the Craigslist baby • 109

proof of errands • 133

the duck in the kitchen • 145

the exchange • 158

when they were young • 181

only in Hollywood • 201

a good egg • 234

the narrative of us • 251

notes for a eulogy

I LIKE WATCHING Jake when he drives, when he's focused on a specific task. It's one of the few times I get to stare—just stare—at his profile, the sharp slant of his nose, the enviable length of his eyelashes. Once, buzzed on champagne at our friend's wedding, I begged him to let me put mascara on them. He refused.

"What's he like?" I ask.

We're an hour into our two-hour drive, and we haven't said much. In the beginning of us, this would have made me nervous, the silence. It doesn't anymore. We're good together. We've embraced that, taken solace in that. The rest of life seems to be a crapshoot, but we're a sure thing. He's not going anywhere and, more importantly, neither am I. My rolling stone of a heart has come to a rest. I've even let him see me pluck the hairs above my lip.

"I don't know. He's a charming type," Jake says. "He's short like me."

When we first started dating, this was an unspoken fact—that Jake is shorter than me; he's not short by average standards, but a few inches beneath my five feet, eleven inches. I used to slouch or stand next to him with one foot out far to the side, leaning down to his height. When he couldn't reach something on the upper shelf of the pantry, I pretended I couldn't either. We're done with that now. I stand tall because I don't want to be hunched over like my grandma when I'm old. And he asks me to get down the vases from the cabinet above the fridge when he brings home flowers.

"Do you look like him?" I ask.

He's biting his nails. He does this when he's nervous. He denies it though. Whenever I witness it and ask what's bothering him, he says, "Nothing. Why?"

"I look just like him. *Just* like him."

He says this like it baffles him, though it shouldn't. We're talking about his father. He didn't grow up calling him "Dad," but he's still his father.

The story isn't original. His parents split up when he was young. I've asked how old he was, and he's never clear—once he said, "I don't know, around ten;" another time he said, "I think I was twelve." He talks about it like it doesn't matter, like the details are meaningless, though they seem like everything to me. My parents are celebrating their thirty-eighth wedding anniversary this year.

After the divorce, Jake didn't see much of his father.

Sometimes he'd swoop in on weekends to take Jake and his sister for ice cream. Then he married a woman named Linda, and Jake stopped hearing from him. Jake was twenty years old, in college, when his father called for the first time in a few years and said he was divorcing Linda. He needed somewhere to stay because she was taking all his money. Jake offered his couch, reluctantly. He thought his father would stay a couple nights, but he stayed a couple months. When he finally moved out, renting a room in a house shared by two college kids, he said he'd never get married again. But then he married Deb.

"What's Deb like?" I ask.

Jake shrugs. "She's loud. Whatever you do, don't try to help her in the kitchen."

"Got it. So she's the overbearing type?"

"That's probably what makes her a good caretaker."

Jake says his father married Deb because he doesn't want to die alone. He was diagnosed with ALS a year ago, right around the time Jake first kissed me.

Amyotrophic lateral sclerosis—I've learned to rattle off the full medical name easily. Most people call it Lou Gehrig's disease, after the famous baseball player who died from it. I'd heard of it before meeting Jake, mostly because I know all things baseball. My dad pitched for the Twins in the seventies before he hurt his shoulder, quit, and then met my mom. He coached my softball teams until I stopped playing sometime before high school.

I'd asked Jake, cautiously, what ALS is, what it does, afraid to make him emotional. He wasn't though. He simply said, "It makes the muscles really weak. It started in my father's legs. He says his legs are, like, dead, paralyzed. And now his arms are going." I tried not to look horror-struck but failed when Jake said, "Eventually, you can't swallow or breathe. You suffocate, in the end."

"And when's the end?" I'd asked.

"Probably two years, tops."

It's not fair, really. His mom is ill too, four stages into pancreatic cancer. They're both in their fifties, his parents—not old enough to die. When he first told me about these cards dealt to him, he'd said, "What are the chances?"

Jake's father invited both Jake and his sister to the cabin, but his sister declined. "I don't want to be that far from mom," she'd told Jake. I was surprised when Jake said he would go—not that he *wanted* to go, but that he would, as a duty. He and his sister agreed not to tell their mom. It would upset her, her son making an effort to visit his father who was never there and his father's third wife.

"Have you told them much about me?" I ask.

I doubt he has. He hardly ever talks to his father. When he does, he uses the same tone he uses on work calls: blunt, direct, authoritative. Jake does something with investment banking that I don't even pretend to find interesting. He's all business on those work calls. Sometimes I wonder what his colleagues and clients would think if they heard how he talks to me, saw how he gives me baby kisses on my cheeks and combs stray hairs out of my eyes.

He looks at me, takes his eyes off the road for a moment.

"I've told them you're my match," he says.

I suppose I don't need them to know anything else. He reaches over, puts his hand on my leg. He turns his eyes back to the road and says, "This probably isn't a good time to tell them we're pregnant, right?"

I used to hate when men said "We're pregnant," as if they were too. But there's something about the way Jake says it, the way he takes ownership of this human growing inside me, that makes me smile. One life going, another on its way— the math of it all could be a comfort. But maybe there is no sufficient comfort at this time, this time that "isn't a good time."

"We're only a few weeks into it. It's bad luck to say anything this early," I say.

I put my hand to my stomach. It doesn't seem real yet, the pregnancy. The only thing keeping me from complete disbelief is the nausea, the saltines on the nightstand.

When we tell people, I think they'll assume it wasn't planned. We're not married, not even engaged. We will be. It just "isn't a good time" to be planning a wedding, the biggest party of our lives. That can wait. Some things can't. We're halfway through our thirties. Jake told me, when I moved in four months ago, that he wanted a family. "Life is too short," he'd said. And I'd said, "Let's have a family."

"They're going to put us to work, just to warn you," Jake says.

Their cabin is near Lake Arrowhead, a weekend getaway from Los Angeles. His father told him he wants his ashes scattered at the cabin, in the backyard under the pine trees. He's leaving the cabin to Deb when he's gone. Jake's worried she'll sell it and when we take our future child to see Grandpa's resting place, Jake will have to knock on the door of strangers and explain: "My father used to own this place. Mind if we walk around back?"

"We'll have to chop some logs, clean up the yard. My father can't do any of that anymore. Obviously. I don't know why they don't hire a gardener."

"That would be admitting defeat," I say.

We hear Jake's mom say this often: "I know I can't drive, but selling the Camry is admitting defeat" and "Buying those damn nutrition shakes is admitting defeat. I can eat real food." Though she can't. She's ninety pounds.

"I was thinking the other day about how I don't know a single thing to say for his eulogy," Jake says.

It's like him—to plan ahead like this, to already be thinking about his speech at the funeral. Ever since I've known him, he's been calendar obsessed, scheduling weekend camping trips and day hikes months in advance, like he's desperate for something to look forward to.

"You have time. You'll think of something," I say. "Maybe this trip will help."

The cabin is at the end of a road so narrow that we have to reverse into a shallow ditch to allow a pickup truck to pass. Ever since we turned off the freeway, Jake's needed GPS to find his way. I wonder how strange it would be to need GPS to find my dad.

"This is it," Jake says, making a quick right up a steep driveway.

The cabin is grander than I expected. I thought it would be a tiny, run-down A-frame. But no. It's a large log-sided house with expansive windows and two stone pillars framing a front door so tall a ten-foot man could walk right through.

"It's huge," I say.

"Deb has money," Jake says, clarifying what he's told me before—that his father never has.

We park at the end of the driveway, triggering the motion sensor lights. A dog barks—first far away, then closer, before appearing at my door. He's a giant black Labrador. I get out, and he sniffs and circles me, tail wagging.

"Hi, puppy," I say, though this dog is old. The hair around his snout is graying. His eyes are foggy. I'm grateful for the presence of an animal—a distraction, an icebreaker, an excuse to go outside for a short walk.

"That's Bruno," someone shouts.

I look up to see a woman who must be Deb. She's walking from the front door toward us. She has hips people call childbearing, though Jake's said she never had kids. Her hair is cut to her shoulders. It's dark—almost black—with strands of gray that seem to be left there for artistic reasons. She has a long nose and small brown eyes.

"And I'm Deb," she says to me. I expect a handshake, but she gives me a hug.

"Deb, this is Alexis," Jake says. He always introduces me to people with my full name, though everyone calls me Alex.

"She's gorgeous," Deb says, hugging Jake. Even after she releases, she leaves her hand on his lower back, like they are close, like they've shared many meals and memories. Jake crosses his arms over his chest and gives me his tight-lipped smile, the one he forces when he's uncomfortable.

"Come, let's go inside," Deb says. We follow her. Jake takes my hand, holds it tight, as if he's scared or presumes I am.

The moment we cross the threshold, a surge of warmth hits us. A fire burns in a stove in the living room, next to huge windows overlooking the forest behind the house. He—Jake's father—is in his wheelchair a few feet from the fire. It's one of those high-powered wheelchairs with the fancy controls. He pushes a button and rolls to us. There's a Ferrari sticker on his headrest.

"Jake," he says, "I'm so happy you guys are here."

"We're glad we could make it," Jake says, as if all the years they didn't see each other were due to logistical problems, snafus, busy schedules.

"You must be Alex," his father says to me, voice booming. "I'm Marco. It's so good to meet you."

"You too," I say.

I come closer, unsure how to approach someone in a wheelchair. He reaches his arms out with the intention of a hug, and I lean down to him, letting him pat my back.

"Sit, sit," Deb says, motioning toward the couch. We obey. "Let me get you two some wine. I have the best pinot noir."

"None for Alex, thanks," Jake says. He does this often—speaks for me, protects me from having to decline. He knows I hate to seem rude.

"So, Alex, what do you do?" Deb asks when she returns with the wine and a bottle of water for me.

"I work at a library," I say.

"Well, doesn't that sound fun," she says, as if I've just told her I make balloon animals.

While Deb and I discuss our favorite books (we have none in common), Jake talks to his father about football standings, the stock market, the carpenter bees making a home in the awning outside—things men discuss to simulate a bond. Jake doesn't look *just* like him. He, the giver of Jake's last name—Mancini—is Italian, through and through: dark hair, dark-brown eyes, olive-toned skin. Jake's sister looks more like him than Jake does. Jake has the dark hair and olive-toned skin, but his mom's Western European ancestry fought for prominence in his eyes. Her blue is mixed in there, giving Jake the emerald green. "He has cat eyes," my sister said once.

"I hear you're a vegetarian," Deb says to me. "I made chicken cacciatore, but I have some pasta with meatless sauce. Is that okay?"

"That's fine. You really don't have to go to any trouble."

She waves me off. "Don't be silly. It's the Jew in me." A laugh comes from deep in her chest—loud and generous. She's one of those people comedians love to have at shows.

"Can I help you with anything?" I ask, out of polite obligation.

"No, no. Sit. Rest. You've had a long drive."

Bruno jumps up on the couch next to me. I pet him, focus intently on that, because I'm not sure what else to do.

"Watch this," Jake's father says. He takes a tennis ball from the cup holder of his wheelchair and tosses it down the hallway. His arms are thin, weak; he's not able to throw it that far. Bruno humors him anyway, jumping up excitedly to retrieve it. He brings it back, dropping it at his owner's feet.

"Oh, Bruno! You know that's not right," Jake's father says, noticeably agitated. He can't reach the ball from his seat. "Remember how I taught you to bring it to my hand?" The dog just looks on, sad and confused, because he's just a dog.

"Jake, bring me the ball," he says. Jake obliges. His father throws the ball again, and Bruno runs down the hallway. When he comes back, Jake's father puts out his hand, desperate, grasping. Bruno drops the ball into his palm.

"Good boy, good boy," Jake's father says. I wonder if this is what consumes his days. I wonder how often he cries.

"So, what have you two been up to?" he asks us. I don't know if he means in the last several years or the last week or two. Jake looks at me and I look at him, our eyes wide and unsure.

"We've been hiking quite a bit. We did Mount Baldy a couple months ago. Mount Whitney before that. And Half Dome, out in Yosemite."

At first, I think Jake's trying to hurt him, this man who can't even walk from his bed to the bathroom in the middle of the night. But that's not his style. That's my style—subtle insults, comments with layers of meaning. Jake's a much better person than I am, truly. He's not reminding his father of his illness; he's telling him that he's doing enough with his strong legs for the both of them.

"That's great, Jake. Really great," his father says. When he smiles, the creases around his eyes deepen and the folds of skin below his lower eyelids arc upward. It looks like his eyes are smiling too. Jake got this from him.

"Jake has taken me on so many adventures," I say. "I complain endlessly on those hikes, but he never does."

Jake puts his arm around me, pulls me into his side. His father looks on at us with pride. When Jake brought up the idea of coming up here, I thought it was for this reason—to give his father some happiness. But Jake had said as we packed the car in the morning, "I don't really want to go. I just want to be able to live with myself after he dies. Is that bad?" I'd said, "No," because I want him to be able to sleep at night. I want him to feel like he did enough, tried enough, so he doesn't get choked up with guilt when our child asks him about the father he hardly knew.

"How's your mother doing?" his father asks. To this question, coming from friends and family, Jake used to say "She's fine" or "As good as can be expected." Now he's tired of that, tired of anything less than the complete truth.

"She's not great."

I rub Jake's back with my hand.

"You're just getting it from all sides," his father says, shaking his head.

Deb brings a bread basket to the dining room table and says, "Food's on." She is one of those people who considers entertaining a hobby. She has special dinnerware and takes time to fold cloth napkins and arrange forks and knives just so.

Jake's father zooms over to the table, to the spot that doesn't have a chair. Deb sits next to him, and we sit across from the two of them. Bruno lies at Jake's father's feet. He must slip him food regularly.

"So, how did you guys meet?" Deb asks, dishing out chicken and pasta onto Marco's plate.

"Last year, we both went out to Joshua Tree for this rock climbing course. Alone," Jake says.

"I can't even tell you what compelled me to try rock climbing. I was just looking for something new, I guess," I say. We love this story—remembering it, telling it.

"On the first day of the course, I saw her and thought she was beautiful. She partnered up with a woman in the class, and I didn't get the nerve to even talk to her until the end of the day."

"He overheard me saying I lived in Manhattan Beach and said he lived there too, so we should join the climbing gym. I mean, you need a partner for rock climbing, so it made sense."

"I met up with her at the climbing gym, and we started going twice a week, just getting to know each other."

It's true—we were just getting to know each other. I hadn't even thought of Jake *that way* at first, because of the height issue. I'd always said I wanted someone taller than me, someone to make me feel small. Then one day, at the gym, I got teary-eyed about my grandma passing away and Jake hugged me. I'd never felt so small, so contained, before.

"I would have thought he'd move faster to snag you. His dad sure did back in 1987," Deb says, with her laugh.

I watch Jake do the calculation in his head—1987. Jake was eight. His parents were still married. Perhaps his father's final months are for confessions, requests for forgiveness.

Jake clears his throat, says, "I didn't realize you two knew each other then."

Deb doesn't seem bothered by the math that verifies an affair. She just goes on:

"We worked in the same office. You know how those things go. We didn't end up together then because you and your sister were just kids. I wasn't interested in being a mom."

I put my hand on Jake's arm. I resent this woman, suddenly, on his behalf. She wanted Jake's father all to herself. She wanted fancy dinners and nights at the theater and spontaneous sex, not boxed mac and cheese and homework assignments and story time before bed. His father doesn't seem offended by this revelation, which makes me resent him too.

"We found our way back to each other though," his father says, smiling at her. Maybe he was never there for Jake because he spent years chasing Deb.

A noodle drops from his father's mouth to his shirt. Deb dips her napkin in a glass of water and starts dabbing at the marinara stain. I'm more judgmental than Jake, more callous. Perhaps it's not my place to say what a proper love story is. Deb bathes Marco, helps him in and out of bed, cooks him chicken cacciatore, cleans his ears with Q-tips. She pulled on the jeans he's wearing and buttoned his collared shirt and tied the laces of his shoes. It would be hard to argue that isn't love. When all is said and done, she got exactly what she wanted—Marco, all to herself.

We eat in silence, except for the sounds of forks against plates and Bruno licking his paw.

"Everything taste okay?" Deb says.

"Great," I say. "Thank you." Jake doesn't say anything.

"Jake, I wanted to talk to you about something. And your

sister too. I wanted to tell her in person, but she can't seem to find the time to meet up," his father says.

"What is it?" Jake says.

"Well, it's about my disease."

I think he's going to tell us it's progressing faster than normal, that time is running out.

"As you may know, most cases of ALS are of undetermined cause, but some are genetic."

"Familial," Deb says, a piece of chicken on the end of her fork.

This is news to me, and I assume it's news to Jake too. We've always talked about ALS as "just one of those awful diseases," something random, not fated.

"We had some testing done to find out the source of mine. My mother died of ALS. I think I've told you that," he says.

"No, you hadn't," Jake says. I can see the muscles in his jaw tighten. I move my hand to his thigh.

"She died when she was fifty-six," Deb says, like she's the keeper of the Mancini family history.

"Not surprisingly, it turns out I have the genetic kind. The familial kind."

"What does that mean?" Jake asks.

"It means you and your sister have a fifty percent chance of having the gene," his father says.

"And if you have the gene, you will develop ALS at some point in your life," Deb says. She's matter-of-fact—too matter-of-fact. My face gets hot.

"So, what? I might inherit this from you?" Jake says.

There is the difference between Jake and me—I would say this with undisguised spite; he says it with perfect calm. I squeeze his thigh.

"There's a chance," his father says.

"A fifty percent chance," Deb says.

You already said that, I want to scream. I want them to shut up. I want to stick my thumbs in my ears like a child. I've always imagined Jake and I growing old together. After years spent raising our child—our children—and then sending them off to college, to their own happy and healthy lives, we would enjoy the quiet again, on the couch, under the blanket my mom knitted and gave us when we moved in together. We'd be grateful for this life, these simple moments we created together. It will have all seemed to have gone by so fast. And, if one of us were to get sick—with one of the many things people get when they live too long—it would be me. He'd take care of me. Because he always does. He buys me soup when I have a cold and checks to ensure it's made with vegetable broth, not chicken. He washes and folds my laundry without me even knowing about it; clean clothes just show up in the drawers. On cold nights, when I've kicked off the quilt in the fit of a dream, he pulls it up and wraps it around me. I pretend to sleep through this, but I know.

I've assumed I'd die first because, frankly, I *want* to die first. Is that selfish? Jake's spoiled my definition of life; it wouldn't be the same without him. I know that because when he stays at his mom's house on the nights her caretaker is off, I wake up in bed with an overwhelming loneliness. I've never been so sappy, almost pathetic, about anyone before. I chose all of my previous boyfriends because I knew I would be fine without them. Loving them didn't carry any risk. I could lose them and go on. I did lose them and go on. When I chose Jake, I felt vulnerable to the possibility that he—the loss of him—could destroy me.

"You could get tested, if you want to know for sure," Deb says.

Jake shakes his head, shakes off the notion of possibly coming to know such a fate. I know Jake. I know he won't want to get tested. He's an optimist, to an almost delusional degree. A positive test result could trigger an identity crisis.

"And it's possible my children—my future children—could carry the gene?" Jake says.

"It's possible," Marco says.

"If you have it, your child would have a fifty percent chance," Deb clarifies.

Shut up, shut up, shut up.

My ears start ringing, the way they did after loud concerts in college. I put both hands on my stomach, apologize silently to our tiny seed of a baby who might be doomed.

We sit there, in mournful silence, until Deb stands from the table and says, "I've got an idea! Let's go out and look at the stars. It's a clear night. It'll be gorgeous, get our minds off all this serious stuff."

We stay seated, not ready for this transition. Then Jake's father reverses his wheelchair, rolling over a squeaky dog toy. Bruno jumps up.

"Great idea, babe," he says.

That bothers me, the "babe." It reminds me of the holiday card they sent us, featuring a photo of them French kissing. Jake had grimaced when he saw it. "I think I see tongue," he'd said.

They make their way to the door. We stand, somewhat reluctantly, and follow. I expect Jake to whisper something to me, but he is quiet. He may not talk to me about any of this for days, a week even. He's more patient than me. He'll sort it out in his head first then come to me. I come to him when nothing is sorted, rely on him to help organize my frantic thoughts.

The night air is chilly. I hide my arms inside my sweater and lean against Jake. Marco and Deb stop in the middle of the long driveway. Deb lies flat on the asphalt and crosses one ankle over the other, gazing up.

"Come on, guys!" she says, waving us over.

"Check this out," Jake's father says. He pushes a button and starts reclining his wheelchair until he's parallel to the ground, like he's at the dentist for a teeth cleaning. "It's like a portable lounge chair." We nod, confirming this single pro in a sea of cons.

The stars are beautiful—brighter and more numerous than they ever are in the city. Jake's hands are in his pockets, his neck tilted up. When the moonlight catches his eyes, I think they seem watery. Maybe it's just the cold air.

"You don't look just like him, you know," I whisper.

Jake takes his hands out of his pockets and wraps his arms around me. I feel his hot breath on my ear as he exhales.

❦

Deb asks us if we mind sleeping in the loft above the living room.

"I'm saving the guest room for a friend of ours who's coming tomorrow," she says. "I don't want to wash the sheets again in the morning."

I try to meet Jake's eyes, to see if he thinks this is as rude as I think it is, but he won't look at me.

"Sure, that's fine," he tells her.

The loft has a full bed, small compared to the king we have at home. The smoke from the stove fire rises to us. It's hot. Our eyes and throats burn. Neither of us sleeps well.

In the morning, we're awakened by voices from the master bedroom, arguing. Their door opens, and I hear Deb go into the kitchen, Marco rolling behind her.

"Look, I wish I could move myself. I wish you didn't have to lift me. I'm sorry your back hurts. Just leave me in bed all day then," he says in a loud whisper.

Deb shushes him and starts pulling out pans, more aggressively than necessary judging by all the clanking.

Jake sits up, yawns exaggeratedly, so as to let them know

we're awake. He hands me my zip-up sweatshirt, I pull on my jeans from yesterday, and we head downstairs. Deb is cracking eggs into a large bowl. We sit at barstools, and it dawns on me that we have a whole day to fill.

"I was thinking you could help me clean out the garage," Jake's father says to him, "and help me fix the lawn mower."

"That would be great, Jake," Deb says. "I can do the mowing, but I can't fix the damn lawn mower." She laughs, seemingly forgetting the spat from moments ago. She must have to do this a lot—forget, move on, allow him the last word because he's dying and she's not.

"Sure, whatever you need," Jake says.

"That means you get to pull weeds with me," Deb says to me, and I try to fake enthusiasm as well as Jake does.

We have a breakfast of omelets, and then Jake follows his father out to the garage. I watch the two of them from the big kitchen window—Jake with his hands stuffed in his pockets, his father zooming along ahead. I miss Jake immediately. Or maybe I'm just dreading the time spent with Deb.

She hands me a trowel. "The weeds are deep," she says.

I follow her out back to the lawn, where Jake's father wants his ashes scattered. It's a nice place for such a thing. Will Jake and I have to discuss each other's wishes at some point? I dread that conversation, or the reason for it.

Deb gets down on her knees, and I do the same. She starts at one end of the lawn; I start at the other. She's right—the weeds are deep. I have to dig into the earth a good three inches before I can tear out the roots. There's such satisfaction when I do though. This project requires no patience; gratification is instant. I can see, right before my eyes, the difference I'm making. I start my own little pile.

A half hour in, we haven't said much to each other, with the exception of a few comments about the sun and how we're getting tans. My fingertips are numb from the prickly weeds, and I'm too shy to ask Deb for a pair of gardening gloves. She has a pair for herself. In other circumstances, I might mention my numb fingertips and the grass stains on the kneecaps of my good jeans. But Deb has a dying man on her watch; she doesn't need my bitching.

"So, are you two talking about getting hitched or what?" she says.

I look in her direction, squinting in the sun. I'm taken aback by the question, the personal nature of it, her lack of hesitation.

"No, why?"

"I just thought it would be nice," she says. "I'm sure Marco would love to see Jake settled down before he passes away."

She wants us to run down the aisle for the sake of Jake's father, though Jake's father has never done much of anything for the sake of his son. I resent her nerve, but then I consider that maybe she doesn't know the whole truth about Marco. Maybe Marco has lied—to her, to himself—about his role as a father. This possibility makes me pity her a little. She thinks she knows him so intimately, so deeply. And here I am, this girl she's just met, and I know something about the love of her life that she never will.

"Life's a bit busy at the moment," I tell her, sidestepping the bigger, harder conversation.

"Well, I'm sure you will get married, at some point. If you know that, it would be nice to do it sooner rather than later."

"I don't think it's up to me," I say, relieved that it truly isn't. If Jake's even thought about proposing, I don't know about it.

"Does it scare you? To know that Jake may get ALS?"

She's still not facing me. She's crouched down, yanking at the ground. She has her own pile of weeds and it's larger than mine, which makes me irrationally mad.

"I guess I don't *know* that yet," I say.

Now she turns around. "It's a fact, though. There's a fifty percent chance."

"I understand."

I leave it at that. I'm not prepared to think about this, let alone talk about it with her.

"If I had to give you one bit of advice," she says, mistaking my silence as a request for that, "get a handicap-ready house when you buy a home. You know, support bars in the shower, by the toilet—the whole nine yards."

I have a brief fantasy of troweling her in the head.

"And you might want to consider not having kids since the gene could get passed on. Or, even if it didn't, you might end up a single parent," she says, her thoughts a runaway train of tragedy. "You could always adopt."

I feel something lurch in my stomach, like a baby kick, though it's far too soon for that. Jake's always said I feel everything in my stomach. Whenever I'm nervous or upset, I tell him I'm queasy or have no appetite. It's like my code language.

I push myself up and dust off my jeans.

"I think I'm going to see what the boys are up to," I say.

I gather my pile of weeds and add it to her pile. When I start walking away, to the front of the cabin where the garage is, Deb doesn't follow. She continues pulling weeds, wrenching them out of the ground forcefully.

When I come around front, Jake and his father are staring at a lawn mower in the driveway. His father is looking on from his wheelchair, his throne, pointing and directing Jake.

"What's going on here?" I say, sidling up to Jake.

"It's broken," Jake says. "The pull string snapped."

"Damn pull string!" his father says, with a startling amount of anger. This may be how he gets through each day—getting mad at inanimate objects because he can.

"We'll go to the hardware store, get another one," Jake says, ever calm. "You can show me how to replace it." It's an offering he's making, this opportunity for a father-son lesson.

"Damn pull string," his father says again, quieter this time.

"We'll leave after this, after I fix the lawn mower," Jake says when we pull into the parking lot of the hardware store.

We are supposed to stay another night.

"They're just going to busy us with weeds and lawn mowers. And besides, they have friends coming in," he says. A moment later: "I thought this would happen."

"What?"

"We'd come and then wonder why we did."

"It's fine, really."

I don't even know what I mean is "fine." That we came? That we're leaving? That I may worry every morning when I wake up, for the next however-many years, that Jake will get a weird feeling in his legs? That he may have a disease that atrophies his body and requires me to care for him before losing him completely? That our child may not have his father? I think we're having a boy. I haven't told Jake that yet, but I do.

"I won't be the father he was—or wasn't, or whatever," Jake says.

"Don't you think I already know what kind of father you'll be?"

He shrugs. "Let's get this stupid pull string."

The hardware store smells musty, like an antique store. A couple of the overhead lights flicker. We're the only customers, and it seems like they haven't had any before us for the last twenty years. An older man with gray stubble on his chin smacks gum at the register. He's listening to the radio, an oldies station, at an absurdly loud volume. He doesn't look up at us. If it were me, I'd ask him where to find a lawn mower pull string, but Jake walks right by and starts exploring the aisles himself. It's this stubbornness that gets us lost on road trips.

I follow him up and down the aisles. I watch him scan the shelves.

"Aha!" he says, grabbing a plastic box containing one lawn mower pull string.

He pays for it at the register, the old man taking his twenty-dollar bill and giving him change without making eye contact.

"Are you sure you want to leave early?" I ask when we're in the car, heading back to the cabin.

"I'm sure. Unless you want to stay. And pull weeds." He smiles. One of his top center teeth is just a bit crooked, attempting to slide in front of the other. Some people would call this a flaw, but I don't. It just reminds me that he refused to wear his retainer as a teenager because, like I said, he's stubborn.

"I'm ready if you are."

We make the last turn, up the road to the cabin.

"He told me he's close to hospice," he says, slowing the car a bit. "They do these tests. A score of one hundred is normal. He was at eighty for a while. He just found out he's around sixty now. And forty is hospice."

"God, Jake," I say.

We pull up to the house. His father is where we left him, his wheelchair parked on the driveway. He looks lonely just sitting there.

"I think I know what to say at the funeral now," Jake says, staring out the front window.

"What?"

"That he would have been a good grandfather," he says. "Because he would."

To make things up to you, I think. Like a do-over.

I don't know if someone who was not a good father can be a good grandfather, but I know Jake needs to believe in the possibility of this redemption. So I say, "That's perfect."

I try to envision the funeral, Jake in a black suit at the podium. It's possible I'll still be pregnant when Marco dies. Deb will be pleased if the baby comes before Marco goes. She will say the baby looks just like him, even if it's not true at all.

Jake jumps out of the front seat and jogs to his father.

"You found it?" his father says, that Mancini smile spreading across his face.

Jake tosses the pull string into his father's lap. His father looks so grateful. Or maybe it's pride. *He's going to cry*, I think.

"Alright, Dad," Jake says. "Let's get this thing going."

what we cannot know

THREE WEEKS AFTER her father died, Deb found out that the very foundation of who she'd been for forty years was a lie.

Her father had died in his sleep at the age of eighty-five—a storybook ending if there ever was one. Deb's mother had passed away the year before. It was sweet, really, the way her father seemed incapable of surviving without his wife.

In the first couple weeks after her father died, Deb couldn't bring herself to go to the house, the same house they'd lived in since she was a child. She wanted to wallow in the denial stage of grief. This wasn't usually her style—wallowing. She prided herself on being a take-the-bull-by-the-horns sort of person, but the loss of her parents hit her harder than she'd expected. She didn't have any other immediate family, no siblings. Her one aunt, her mother's sister, had died some years ago. She felt suddenly and acutely alone. Grieving, she realized, was meant to be done in a group, with people sharing memories and tears and embraces.

Deb had never made much time for friends. She was a marketing director for a Fortune 500 pharmaceutical company and was always traveling for work. If she got seriously sick, she couldn't think of anyone who would come visit her in the hospital. Except for Marco. But when they'd talked a few years ago, she swore—to herself and to him— that it was the last time.

When she finally went to the house, she came armed with cleaning supplies and trash bags, determined to sort through everything as quickly as possible. She'd already contacted a realtor about selling the place. The realtor was young and eager; he would keep her focused on the task at hand.

She started with the kitchen because she thought it'd feel good to throw away everything in the fridge and pantry. She wasn't prepared to encounter her father's wall calendar, full of his scribbles, plans marked on days weeks away. She packaged up some dishware to drop off at the Salvation Army then moved on to the office. She figured she'd go through the filing cabinet, pull as many relevant documents as she could find.

The cabinet was stuffed with papers—old utility bills, receipts for purchases made two decades ago, handwritten notes that no longer made sense. There was a whole drawer dedicated to recipes. Deb's parents had owned a deli—Alter's, named after her father. Her mother created the menu and instructed the cooks on all the preparations. Her corned beef was named the Best Corned Beef in Los Angeles by an obscure food magazine. Deb put several of the folders in her oversize purse, telling herself she would learn the recipes, after so many years telling her parents she wanted nothing to do with the deli business. She could almost hear her father chuckling.

When she looked outside, the sun was starting to set. Somehow, three hours had passed, and she hadn't made any real progress. She sighed at the thought of the work ahead and decided to give up for the day. This wasn't usually her style either—giving up.

She went home to the Brentwood condo that she shared with her cat. This existence of hers always saddened her mother. She wanted nothing more than for Deb to "settle down." It was less about Deb finding true love than it was about grandchildren, though. Her mother always said things like, "Women these days are waiting far too long to have children. You don't want to miss out." But the thing was, Deb *did* want to miss out. She'd never wanted kids, had always seen herself as more of a "career woman." When her friends started having kids, Deb stopped having friends. She just couldn't bring herself to fake interest in the monotonous details of these tiny, needy humans. That said, she didn't have anything against having a husband. It was just that, as Marco had told her once, the timing was never right.

After she fed the cat, she headed to the wine bar down the street and ordered a bottle of zinfandel that the bartender described as "liquefied jam." He was her favorite bartender, quite obviously gay, with perfectly plucked eyebrows and hair gelled into a trendy mohawk. She sipped while her phone buzzed with messages from work. She had a big presentation the next day, the details of which escaped her after her second glass.

She took one of the recipe folders out of her purse, started flipping through the pages, mostly to see her mother's notes about cook times and tweaks. Behind the matzo ball recipe was a page torn from an old newspaper, folded into a perfect square. Deb unfolded it carefully; the paper was yellowed and delicate, like it might disintegrate in her hands. It was a *Los Angeles Times* article, dated December 15, 1962.

Deli Baby Finds a Home
By Rosemary Witten

LOS ANGELES—After months of waiting, the baby girl known as the Deli Baby has a home. Mary Simpson, spokesperson for the Children and Family Services Division (CFSD) of the California Department of Social Services (CDSS), confirmed that the baby girl has been adopted by the couple who found her at the back door of their deli one year ago.

"It was three weeks before Hanukkah. We thought she was a gift to us," said Karen Weintraub, the baby's adoptive mother. "The finalization of the adoption is this year's gift."

The newborn girl was abandoned on December 5 of last year. The Weintraubs found her in the early morning hours when they were opening Alter's Deli for the day.

"We'd wanted a baby for a long time. It was just the strangest thing," Alter Weintraub said. "I never thought I believed in fate, but maybe I do."

The baby girl was found wrapped in a sweatshirt, wearing only a diaper. A note was found with the baby: "I wish I could take care of her. I know you will. Thank you."

After months of investigation and many false leads, police were unable to locate the baby's mother. The baby was placed in foster care while the state determined the best course of action.

"We had been on a list with an adoption agency for a year at that point," Mrs. Weintraub said. "We decided we wanted to adopt the baby who was literally placed at our feet."

"It's an unprecedented thing," Simpson said. "We've had abandoned babies before, of course. But we've never had them adopted by the people who found them."

The Weintraubs named their daughter Deborah Lynn. With the adoption final, even if Deborah's mother returns, she will be denied custody.

"There's a waiting period for a reason," Simpson

said. "That time has passed. It's our hope at the CDSS that Deborah has a wonderful life with her new family."

"I pray that this is the most drama and pain she will ever endure," Mrs. Weintraub said. "It relieves me that she will not remember any of it."

Deb read the article a second time, then a third, then a fourth. She sat still, heavy, unable to move, as if the blood in her veins had turned to cement.

"You doing okay?" the bartender asked.

She heard him, but it sounded as if he were very far away. Her head felt too heavy to lift.

"What?"

"You doing okay?"

"Yes."

He left her alone. Her head spun, with wine or shock. How could they have kept this from her? She felt an intense anger toward them then guilt for the anger. They were dead, after all. They had nothing to say for themselves.

Maybe they were trying to protect her from knowing she'd been left—discarded, really—at the back door of their deli. Maybe they thought it would have been too painful for her to know such a thing. Maybe it *would* have been too painful. Maybe she would have been screwed up. Maybe she never would have made anything of her life. Maybe her parents did her a favor.

Still, though, they'd cheated her of the opportunity to know who she truly was.

The bartender refilled Deb's glass.

"Is this a 'heartbreak bottle'?" he asked, putting air quotes around his term.

Deb couldn't help but think of Marco again. She wanted—*needed*—to tell someone about this, and he was the only person she could think of who would care more about her than about the sensational story of it all. She couldn't call him, though. She was just having a moment of weakness, exacerbated by the wine.

"In a way," Deb told the bartender. Because, in a way, her heart *was* broken.

"Oh, sweetie," the bartender said. "We've all been there."

She wanted to tell him that he likely hadn't been where she was, but he wasn't the person to hear her story. He set a dish of nuts on the counter next to her glass and walked away.

Deb remembered once, when she was about twelve, crying to her mother about how tall she was. At nearly five feet, nine inches tall, she towered over the boys in class and hated it.

"You and Dad aren't tall," she'd said.

It was true. Her parents weren't tall. They were short. Her father was barely five foot five, her mother barely five feet. And they weren't just short, but they were small, in general. Petite. Deb had always been big-boned.

"You're right, we aren't tall. My grandpa was tall though," her mother had told her.

"But why do *I* have to be so tall?"

Her mother attempted a look of sympathy, jutting out her bottom lip.

"My dear, life has so many questions," she'd said, stroking Deb's cheek. "Sometimes we have to be okay with what we cannot know."

Her mother did this often—made big, philosophical statements. Deb always rolled her eyes.

Now she thinks what her mother should have said was "Sometimes you have to be okay with what I don't want to tell you."

Deb met Marco when she was just twenty-five, starting her first real job at Genixer, a small pharmaceutical company specializing in chemotherapy drugs. Deb started as an assistant to a marketing director, which meant she was in meetings throughout the day, taking notes. She noticed Marco right away.

Marco was a product manager, a few years older than her and the most attractive man on her team. He reminded her of Ponch on the TV show *CHiPs*—a full head of black hair, twinkling brown eyes, a charming smile, fluorescent white teeth. He was shorter than she was, but he carried himself like he was the tallest person in the room. When she felt the buzz of attraction in her chest, she did what she always did—checked his ring finger. And there it was: proof that he'd been claimed by someone else.

She didn't see any harm in fantasizing. Whenever they were in meetings together, Deb stared at Marco's olive-toned hands and imagined them running up her legs. She hiked up her skirt when she sat near him, hoping he'd take notice of her legs. Her mother always said they were her best asset.

Deb couldn't rationalize spending money on takeout, so she brought her lunch to work every day. Marco brought his lunch too. A few weeks into the job, he came into the break room just as she was sitting to eat her sandwich and said, "Hey, Deb, mind if I join you?"

She couldn't believe he knew her name. She hoped she wasn't blushing when she said, "Sure."

His lunch was in a brown paper bag. When he opened it, he seemed surprised at its contents: "Roast beef," he said. Deb guessed his wife packed his lunches.

They chitchatted about work and where they'd gone to college (UCLA for him, USC for her). He was one of those people who didn't break eye contact during a conversation. Deb found it flattering—he seemed so interested in everything she had to say—but also unnerving. She kept finger-combing her hair behind her ear nervously.

Over the next several weeks, they made a habit of meeting in the break room. It wasn't a planned thing, or not admittedly so; he just kept showing up right at 12:30 p.m., when she was there. She found it easy to talk to him, which was something. She didn't find it easy to talk to most people. He wanted to know her thoughts—on politics, food, religion, books, movies, everything. She'd never felt so *seen* before. He told her about his marriage. He and his wife had been together since high school. They had two kids, a girl and a boy, both in elementary school. "It's hard on a marriage, having kids," he'd said, breaking eye contact as he looked down at his sandwich. In retrospect, this is when the affair started—with this confession.

Their lunch dates turned into happy hours at the bar across the street from the Genixer building. The happy hours turned into kissing in the parking lot. Kissing in the parking lot turned into Marco coming back to Deb's apartment. He could never stay long, for obvious reasons, and Deb didn't mind, really. A girlfriend of hers had told her once, "You always go for the unavailable men." She didn't disagree.

The affair went on for nearly a year—Marco telling his family he had to work late, Deb telling herself she wasn't a home-wrecker. One afternoon, they each left work early, around four o'clock, so they could have an extra hour at her apartment. They made love then lay together naked in her bed, staring up at the ceiling fan as it whirred.

"I've been thinking," Marco said.

Deb's heart started beating faster, anticipating his words. She'd been bracing for this—the day he would say, "We can't do this anymore."

That's not what he said though.

"What if I left Joan?" His wife, Joan. "She would be happier, in the end. We're not happy together. The kids see it. You and I, we could get a place together. I'd have the kids every other week. It sounds kind of ideal. I'd get a chance to miss them, wouldn't be so exhausted by them. They'd love you."

He leaned into her, kissed her cheek. She couldn't help but smile, but something nagged at her—the kids, the idea of herself as a stepmom.

"Really?" was all she managed to say.

"I'm serious."

She rolled away from him, sat up, swung her legs over the side of the bed. She pulled her robe off the chair and draped it around herself.

"I don't know. I just . . . I'm not sure I'm the mothering kind," she said.

"You'd be a wonderful mother," he said, with that charming smile, those shining teeth.

She saw it then—he assessed her not just as a lover, a girlfriend, but as a mother. She'd never wanted to be assessed that way.

"I need to think about it," she told him. She had a hard time looking at him.

He got out of bed, came to her, wrapped his arms around her middle. He was short enough to rest his head on her shoulder, and she suddenly found this embarrassing.

"You take all the time you need," he said.

She started making up excuses for why she couldn't get together after work—she was meeting a girlfriend for drinks, she'd signed up for an aerobics class, she had a migraine. It wasn't that she didn't love him; it was that she knew they couldn't be together in the way she wanted. She wanted the luxury of being obsessed with only each other. The moment he'd made it clear she couldn't have that, the moment he'd mentioned Joan and the kids, she retreated—not to hurt him, but to protect herself. He got the hint and wasn't shy about confronting her.

"I scared you, didn't I?" he said when he found her in the lunchroom, a half hour later than their usual time.

"You didn't scare me," she said. She felt light-headed. "You just reminded me of reality."

He nodded solemnly. "I understand," he said. "Maybe the timing's just off."

He spoke as if there was a destiny to them, as if they would come together again, later. He'd always been a romantic.

"Maybe," she said, humoring him.

"I'll trust the universe on this one." He looked upward, toward the sky, smiled, then added, "Just don't be a stranger, okay?"

She was a stranger, though, for her own sake. She started applying to other jobs, knowing it would be too hard to see him every day at the office. It didn't take long to find something—an up-and-coming pharma company hired her after one interview.

Deb assumed she'd never see Marco again, that he would always be her soul-mate-in-another-life. She couldn't even think of him as "the one that got away" because he was never really hers.

Two years into trying to forget him, he called.

"My divorce is final," he said.

Her heart was hammering in her chest. She'd been standing when she answered the phone; now she had to sit.

"Took longer than expected, but it's final. I told myself I wouldn't call you until it was final. I think we should try again, Deb."

She didn't know what to say, so she was quiet. He kept talking, stating his case with a speech that sounded practiced. He said there would be no pressure to move in together, no pressure to be a stepmom to his kids. They would date; they would enjoy each other. The universe—it was always "the universe" with him—would figure out the rest.

It was like something out of a movie. Or it could have been, if she wasn't living with an international business attorney named Greg.

"Marco, stop," Deb said, interrupting him, finally. "I'm with someone."

She had to say it again before he understood.

"Just my luck." He gave a little laugh. "I just can't seem to get it right."

"Get what right?"

"The timing."

Deb and Greg dated for five years. True to her modus operandi, he was wonderfully unavailable. He worked late, traveled a lot. Or that's what he said when he was gone so often. Then she found out he'd been cheating on her for months. Deb was too proud to be devastated. She pretended not to care, cast him out of her life as if he'd meant nothing. She did care, though. When she got into bed alone at night, she tried to read, but tears blurred her vision. The tears weren't about missing him as much as they were about hating herself for being so stupid. She considered her private pain to be punishment for her past role as the mistress. She kept thinking about that past role, about Marco, about getting the timing right.

She called him, or tried to. He wasn't at the same number. This, she thought, was the universe telling her to stop her silly ruminating and move on. But then, just a few months after the phone call attempt, she was at work, reviewing résumés for field sales representatives, and his came across her desk. Marco Mancini.

When she called the phone number listed at the top of

the résumé, she cleared her throat, planning to put on a fake voice and say, "Hello, Mr. Mancini, I'm calling about the résumé you submitted to Revon Pharmaceuticals." But it was a woman's voice that answered.

"Hello?" the voice repeated while Deb did her best to collect herself.

"Oh, hi. Sorry. I'm looking for Marco Mancini. Do I have the wrong number?"

"No, this is it. This is his wife. What can I do for you?"

Deb hung up. It was a reflex, a hammer-to-the-knee kind of reaction.

He'd married again. She couldn't believe it. She'd thought, stupidly, that he'd be waiting for her, that their togetherness hinged on her readiness and nothing else. She was absurdly and irrationally angry at him, this man she hadn't even seen in person for eight years.

She spent the next few years working her way to a management position at Revon, dating occasionally, living in the same apartment, becoming something of a wine connoisseur. She thought of Marco from time to time, just wondering what had become of his life. Social media allowed her to entertain these curiosities.

Facebook was becoming increasingly popular and, given her position in the marketing world, she created a profile to familiarize herself with the platform that everyone was calling "the future." He was the first person she searched for. There were only two people on Facebook with his name—

one in Italy, one in Los Angeles. She couldn't help but click.

His profile was public, but it was obvious he didn't use the site much. She'd wanted to see his wife, to know whom he'd chosen in her place, but there were no photos, aside from a profile picture that looked to be a corporate photo, like something on a badge he wore clipped to his belt at work.

She decided to send him a message, just to say hello, scratch the itch that kept nagging her. It had been more than a decade since they'd had their fling. That's how she'd relegated it in her mind—a fling, nothing more. Her note was short, and when she read it back after clicking "send," she chastised herself for using too many exclamation marks.

He wrote back the very next day, with his own plethora of exclamation marks. He said he couldn't believe they'd reconnected. He said they should meet up for a drink. He gave her his phone number. She didn't ask about the wife. She wanted to pretend she didn't exist, for just a little while.

They decided to meet at their old bar, the one across the street from the Genixer building, or what the Genixer building used to be (it had become an apartment complex; the company had sold to a pharma giant some years earlier). The bar had a different name but looked the same inside. Deb arrived first, got a table in the back, ordered a gin and tonic. When he walked in, it was as if no time had passed. He looked exactly the same, and she had the same fluttery feeling she did way back then.

"My god, you don't age," he said, hugging her, his hand lingering on her arm as they took each other in.

"Trust me, I do," she said. "You, on the other hand, don't."

When they sat, he placed his hands on the table and she saw the wedding ring.

"So," she said, trying not to stare at it, "catch me up."

"We're separated. Linda and me. That's my wife—Linda."

Deb felt her cheeks reddening, knew her eagerness was obvious.

She should have kept their meeting short and platonic. She should have paid her part of the bill after one drink and gone on her way. But that's not what Deb did. Instead, she changed the subject, and they continued talking—flirting, really—until the bar closed. Deb had never been the last person in a bar before, had never seen the lights go on. They weren't drunk, but they were tipsy and giddy.

"Well, I guess we should go back to my apartment," Deb said when they stood in the street outside. She surprised herself with the proposition, knew she would be ashamed of herself the next day.

If Marco had hesitated at all, she would have sobered up in seconds. But he said, "Wouldn't want to break with tradition."

When they made love, it was slower and less frenzied than when they were younger, when he'd had to be home for dinner by seven o'clock. She fell asleep next to him, a privilege she'd never had before. She thought maybe they could go to breakfast, talk about the timing finally being right.

He was snoring lightly when she heard his phone buzz. It was on the floor next to his side of the bed, vibrating against the hardwood. This was back when not everyone had a cell phone, when they were still novel. Deb got out of bed and tiptoed to the phone. The name "Linda" flashed on the screen. The phone stopped buzzing, but then it started again, the same name flashing. Deb felt sick.

"Hey," Marco said, opening his eyes slowly. He shifted his gaze down, to the phone.

"Your wife is calling," Deb said.

At the mention of her, he sat up in bed, as if a bolt of electricity had shot right through him.

"Shit," he said.

Deb knew, with just that one word, that what he had told her—that they were separated—was a lie.

He grabbed the phone and let himself out the door, into Deb's side yard. He was naked.

She watched him pacing back and forth, talking with animated expressions. It was cold outside. His penis looked so small. Deb was disgusted—with herself, with him, with all of it.

She pulled on a pair of jeans and a sweatshirt and went into the kitchen, started brewing coffee as if it were any other day. Ten minutes later, he appeared before her, wearing his boxer shorts now.

"Deb," he said. "It's not what you think."

"That's what every liar says."

"We're not separated, but we almost are. We've been having issues for months. I don't know why I told you we were separated. I guess I wanted us to be. I wanted you and me to have a chance, finally."

"Just stop, okay?" Deb ran her hands through her hair. "I don't care. Just leave. And when she finally leaves you, don't call me. Ever again. Got it?"

He nodded solemnly then went to her bedroom to gather his things. She turned to the sink, pretended to be washing dishes, so she wouldn't have to see him when he let himself out. When she heard the door click, confirming his exit, she threw her mug at the wall. She wanted it to shatter into a million pieces, but it just cracked in two.

The mohawked bartender lifted the bottle of Zin in the air, examining its emptiness in the bar lights.

"It really was like liquefied jam," Deb said.

He winked then sauntered away to a group of women waving him over.

Deb still had Marco's number in her contacts list. She'd done a few purges of phone numbers over the years, deleting people from her life, but she'd never deleted him.

"Just call," the bartender said.

He had returned and was a few feet away from her, mixing

a trendy-looking pink cocktail. The contemplation must have been obvious on Deb's face. She smiled to herself, thinking how Marco would find it funny if she did call and said, "A bartender with a mohawk told me to call you, so here I am."

She took a deep breath and did it. Maybe it was because of the bartender. Maybe it was because of the wine. Maybe it was because the news she'd learned was just too much not to share with someone.

The phone rang two times before he answered.

"Deb?" he said.

He hadn't deleted her either.

"It's me," she said. She was trying hard to keep her voice even. She didn't want him to know she'd needed alcohol to call him.

"You have no idea how many times I've hoped you'd call," he said.

She laughed, in spite of telling herself not to get charmed again.

"Let me guess—you're married?" she said.

"Negative. You?"

"Negative," she said.

"I don't believe it. You must have a stable of eager boyfriends then," he said.

"Again, negative."

"Well, how about that."

She didn't know what to say, so she just blurted out the truth: "I needed to talk to someone, and I thought of you."

"Is everything okay?" he asked, his voice full of concern.

"Yes. I mean, nobody died. Well, my dad died, but that's not why I'm calling," she said. She felt her face redden. "Are you still in Los Angeles? Can you meet for lunch . . . tomorrow, maybe?"

Lunch seemed safe. Deb felt she was at an age when safe mattered, when her heart could take only so much.

"Even if I wasn't in Los Angeles, I'd be there."

Their lunch lasted until four o'clock, when the winter sky started to turn gray. They talked about everything—their loves and losses. He was, in fact, divorced, for the second time. His kids were grown, of course. His son, Jake, worked at an investment firm; his daughter, Charlotte, was a schoolteacher.

"Charlotte and I talk on the phone sometimes. I feel like I'm just a line item in her day planner, but it's still nice to hear from her," he said. "Jake and I . . . well, you know how father-son relationships can be."

"I've heard," Deb said.

Deb didn't have any ex-spouses or children to discuss, so she talked mostly about work. She assumed it was boring, but Marco nodded along like he was fascinated.

"I always knew you'd be one of the higher-ups," he said.

He'd never really climbed the ladder. He'd jumped from job to job, always making a middle-of-the-road salary.

"Anyway," she said. "What I wanted to talk to you about—well, it's kind of strange."

She took the article out of her purse and handed it to him. She watched his eyes scan it. When he was done, he leaned back in his chair and put his hands behind his head.

"Wow," he said. "That's wild."

"To put it simply."

"I can't even imagine how you must be feeling," he said.

"I hardly know how to feel."

"Do you think she's still out there? The woman who left you—"

"My mother, you mean?"

"Well, yes, I guess that's what she'd be," he said.

At first, Deb had been so shocked by her parents' lies that she hadn't considered whether her mother was alive, in the world somewhere. She supposed it was possible. When she imagined a woman leaving a baby, she imagined a teenager, someone too scared to know any better. That teenager would be in her mid to late fifties now. Deb had friends that age.

"I have no idea," she said. "Maybe."

He leaned forward, put his elbows on the table.

"You have to find out, don't you?" he said. "Unless you don't want to, of course. I guess I shouldn't presume you'd want—"

"I feel like I have to try to find her. I can't just . . . not."

He rubbed his hands together conspiratorially.

"Can I help?" he asked.

She hadn't thought of this—him offering his help in any way. She'd just wanted to tell another human being this odd story.

"Sure," she said. "I guess."

They decided to meet for lunch every Saturday to work on what they called "The Case." It was a friendly thing. They didn't kiss or even touch. That feeling was still there between them—that chemistry or spark or electricity or whatever else love songs called it. That hadn't changed; they had.

They started by contacting the *Los Angeles Times*. They found out that several articles had run about the Deli Baby. It was, apparently, a big local story at the time. They read through all the old articles, all written by Rosemary Witten. There were no additional clues in the articles.

Rosemary Witten had died. Mary Simpson, the woman mentioned in the articles as the spokesperson for the Children and Family Services Division was also dead. They looked through the CFSD records. Everything about Deb's adoption was well documented, but there was no information about the mysterious person who had left Deb at the deli.

Marco requested the police reports. They pored over the pages, looking for any leads. The police had done all the right things: They had asked Deb's parents and all the other workers at the deli if they had been in contact with any pregnant girls or women. They had knocked on doors in the surrounding neighborhoods. The assumption was that the person who had left Deb was local. It had to be someone familiar with the deli, perhaps even familiar with the fact that the Weintraubs desperately wanted a baby. The police even looked into the possibility that the Weintraubs had stolen Deb and made up the story about finding her. But a frantic mother would have come forward, looking for her missing newborn, and that didn't happen.

"I think we're at a dead end," Deb said, exhaling so hard that her bangs fluttered.

"Maybe not," Marco said with that smile of his. "I was able to get the lead investigator's phone number. Found it online. He's still alive."

Marco made the call, his phone sitting in the center of the table so they both could hear. A woman answered. Marco did the talking. That was his role on "The Case."

It took nearly five minutes to convince the poor woman that they were not telemarketers. It took another five minutes to explain why they were calling.

"Oh, right, my father told me about that case," the woman said.

So she was the lead investigator's daughter.

"Is he available? We just have a few quick questions. We're wondering if he had any hunches that he didn't include in the official reports," Marco said.

Deb leaned forward, getting hopeful.

"Gosh, I wish he could help you," the woman said.

Deb sat back, prepared for the coming disappointment.

"My father's had Alzheimer's for the past few years. He doesn't even remember he was a detective," the woman said.

"I'm so sorry," Marco said, with apparent heartache on her behalf. Deb was thinking only of her own sadness; she was glad Marco was the face of their operation.

"No, I'm sorry," the woman said.

And, just like that, their final lead led nowhere.

"Life is cruel," Deb said when Marco ended the call. She was thinking of Alzheimer's and abandoned babies and lost love.

Marco reached across the table and took her hand in his, without hesitation. It was the most intimate physical contact they'd had in years. He looked into her eyes and didn't say anything. In that silence, she wondered if maybe the universe—the infamous universe—had given her the article not so she could find her biological mother, but so she could find her way back to Marco.

Marco squeezed Deb's hand. She felt her nose tingle with coming tears, but she managed to look up.

"My mom said something to me once," she said. She would always refer to her as her mom, not her "adoptive mom." She may not have birthed Deb, but she'd given her life.

"She said, 'We have to be okay with what we cannot know.'"

Marco's own eyes welled up. He took her other hand in his, squeezed again. When he smiled, she noticed the lines etched around his eyes. They were both older now. Older and wiser, people say, though their wisdom was debatable. If she were wise, she would thank him for his help, wish him a fond farewell, and keep in touch through annual holiday cards and phone calls on birthdays.

"My dear," Marco said, "there is so much we cannot know."

days that used to be

BILL HASN'T GIVEN much thought to his wedding ring before. It's just part of his finger, almost melded into the flesh. But, while sitting in traffic on the freeway, he finds himself transfixed by it, thinking it strange there on his finger. He starts to pull at it, progressing to yanking, heart beating faster as he realizes it won't budge. He knows he's taken it off before—that time they went scuba diving in Florida, that time Wendy made him take that pottery class with her. He doesn't remember it being especially difficult. Maybe he's gained weight in his fingers over the years. But Wendy has seen to it that he hasn't gained much weight anywhere else. Do people fatten up in their fingers, exclusively? He tries twisting it off, thinking that's a better method than the pulling, but that only aggravates the fine, usually undisturbed finger hairs. He even spits onto his hand, hoping the saliva will provide enough lubrication, but the knuckle presents a barrier he just can't overcome.

When he gets home, Wendy's making dinner, a stir-fry that has become the Tuesday Night Stir-Fry after he mistakenly said he liked the recipe two months ago. It has a disproportionate amount of soy sauce, among other problems, and he hates it, enough to eat a Snickers on the way home to satisfy himself.

"What are you doing?" Wendy asks as he rifles through the cabinets.

"I need some oil."

"For what?"

"I just want to get my wedding ring off."

"Why?"

"It's just bothering me that I can't get it off."

"Why does it matter? You've had it on for thirty-five years."

"I know. Isn't that strange? What if the skin underneath is decaying?"

"Bill, you're freaking me out."

He became a Bill somewhere along the way. Just like their heading-for-eternity marriage, he doesn't know how that happened. He used to be a Billy. Sometime after his fortieth birthday, Billy didn't seem appropriate anymore.

"Wendy, please, where's the olive oil?"

She walks to a cupboard he's already searched and hands him the bottle. He twists off the cap and pours the oil on his hands as he stands over the sink. He rubs his hands together frantically, continuing to pull and yank and twist.

"Is this like cold feet a few decades too late?" she jokes.

"I can't get it over the knuckle," he says, panicky, yanking harder, his finger turning a strange shade of purple as the finger flesh squeezes up against the knuckle, accordioned like the folds of skin on a shar-pei dog.

Wendy dishes rice onto his plate and takes the chicken off the stove.

"Zuma," she calls, putting a few of the chicken chunks into a doggy dish by the kitchen table. Zuma is their fourteen-year-old Labrador retriever. "Can you get the dog? Her hearing's getting worse by the day."

She throws a dishrag at him, implying he should dry his hands, forget whatever ridiculous midlife crisis ring paranoia he's exhibiting. As he wipes off the oil, Zuma walks in, her long nails clinking against the tile floor. They stopped trimming her nails months ago. Zuma has become bony, almost too bony to look at; they strum her ribs like guitar strings when they pet her. Her head hangs low, accentuating her pointy shoulders, and the flesh of her legs has disappeared, leaving behind twigs unfairly expected to carry the weight of her body. She is falling apart at an accelerated pace, has some kind of boil or tumor on her back, disease of the gums, and cataracts in her eyes. The other day, Bill said to Deb and Marco, their dog park friends, "Zuma doesn't have long," hoping they'd disagree. He shouldn't have expected them to have much sympathy; Marco's in a wheelchair, dying of ALS, after all. Deb shrugged, somewhat carelessly, and said,

"You've had so many good years with her," and Bill had to will tears away.

"Come here, sweetie," Wendy says, taking Zuma by the collar and leading her to her dish. Wendy always feeds Zuma first.

They sit at the dinner table, eating in silence, Bill resenting the baby corns in the stir-fry. He knows he's mentioned at some point that he's opposed to baby vegetables, categorically. He watches Wendy eat, opening her mouth wide for each bite, as if she's playing the airplane game with her food, the spoon propelling toward her face. Bill looks to Zuma. He used to slip her food under the table, but she isn't eating anymore, not even when he specially cooks eggs for her on Sunday mornings.

"Bill," Wendy says, looking up from her plate, "do you still want to be married to me?"

He chews his undercooked piece of broccoli slowly, using adherence to manners as an excuse to stall in giving the expected immediate "yes" response. He's never really considered such a question. They are married. That's it. Wanting disappeared from the picture long ago. They're in it for the reputed long haul, have a silent understanding that it's too late to turn back.

"What do you mean? Why would you ask that?" he says, defensive, pretending it's absurd for her to even doubt him.

"I don't know. This wedding ring thing is weird, don't you think? You've never been concerned about it before. I don't even notice mine now."

"But that's the point. You don't even *notice* it. Don't you think being married is something one should *notice*?"

She shrugs, implying they are beyond the "noticing" phase, beyond being appreciative of each other. They have settled into a sort of apathy, expectations for perpetual marital excitement and harmony exhausted sometime after the notorious seven-year mark.

"What if we're just being complacent?" he says.

"Where is this coming from? Did you meet someone?" she asks, tone growing angrier, higher-pitched.

"You can't be serious."

There was a time when he wished he'd meet someone, have an affair, a reason to leave behind monotony. There were bad years when he probably would have cheated if someone had come along. But someone didn't. Now he's sixty-four years old and nearly bald, with a languishing sex drive.

"I don't know, Bill," she says. She always uses his name when she's mad. Then: "Are you not happy?"

He hasn't considered that either.

"With me, I mean," she adds.

They don't talk anymore, not like they used to. There are the usual "how-was-your-day" questions, typical discussions of weather and the plots of television shows. More than anything, they grunt at each other: "Hungry?" "Eh." "Tired?" "Er." They have regressed to some kind of caveman existence, having sex occasionally for the sake of primal need, but nothing else. He loves her, he does. But maybe love is overrated, a side effect of being together as long as they have. Does he *like* her? He doesn't know, and isn't not knowing such a thing inherently problematic? Reason for a divorce? Like "irreconcilable differences"—"forgot if spouse is likable"?

On paper, divorce would be fairly uncomplicated. They don't have kids. They've paid off their mortgage. They could just sell their house, take their proceeds, and go their separate ways. He'd have to risk cutting off his finger if the ring continued to be difficult. And, of course, there would be the issue of Zuma. Who would get custody?

"Well?" Wendy asks, pushing individual grains of rice across her plate with her fork.

"I don't know," he says.

"You don't know if you're happy with me? Jesus, Bill, that's pretty *basic*, don't you think?"

"It is pretty basic."

She rolls her eyes, stands, takes her plate to the sink. She stops in front of the dishwasher.

"Oh no, Zuma!"

"What is it?" Bill asks, turning his head toward her.

"She shit again."

The vet had told them Zuma is losing control of her bowel movements. He'd said her organs are failing and that they could put her down or wait it out. They'd decided to wait it out.

"It's a wet one," she says, as if it's his fault.

"Don't get mad at me about it. She's just old. Do you want me to yell at you when you start crapping your pants?" he says.

"I'm starting to think you won't stick around that long."

With that, she throws a plastic grocery bag and some paper towels at him—the supplies needed to clean up after Zuma's geriatric mess.

"Why do I have to do it? I did it last time."

"Because I say so," she says. "I'm going to dye my hair."

She walks past him, gathering her shoulder-length hair into a haphazard ponytail. She cuts her hair shorter every year. It used to be so long—long and dark brown. She gets her brown from a bottle now, and the shade just isn't quite right. After a few weeks, the gray strands return, reminding him of all that's changed.

Bill gets on his knees, cleans the floor, thinking of his wife with her plastic shower cap on her head, the bathroom smelling like chemicals, brown stains on the tile floor, where she's squirted and missed her scalp. He hates when the dye gets in the grout. He decides in that moment that he doesn't *like* her; he'll choose "irreconcilable differences" after all.

He met Wendy in 1978, at a concert at the LA Forum. Neil Young was playing with Crazy Horse. It was October, right before Halloween. Bill (then twenty-seven-year-old Billy) was humming along to "The Loner," cigarette resting on his lips, when he turned to his right and saw Wendy with hair down to her hips, body swaying back and forth in that seventies way. He smiled at her and she smiled back, and he saw something in that grin—in the rise of her cheekbones, in that little space between her two front teeth—that made him believe in love at first sight.

When the show ended, she sauntered over to him, hair swinging in her wake. He thought about what it would be like to have his hand on her back, to feel those soft hairs graze against his fingers.

"You got another one of those?" she asked him, playfully flicking his cigarette.

"I don't know. Are you even old enough to smoke?" he teased.

She rolled her eyes. "I'm nineteen."

"Well, I'll share if you've got a minute to catch some fresh air and tell me your name."

She smiled and nodded, understanding the politics of flirtation, and allowed him to guide her through the crowd, his hands on her shoulders.

They leaned against the wall outside, looked up at the cloudless sky.

"Wendy," she said.

"Billy," he said. He was already pressing his palms against hers, interlocking his fingers with hers, so there was no formal shaking of hands.

"Big Neil Young fan?"

"The biggest," she said, the tips of her fingers drawing meaningless shapes on his palms.

"I thought I was."

"Well, I'm stealing the title from you."

He loved her sass, how it came hissing out from a small gap between her teeth. Her eyes were big and sky blue, not innocent, maybe even sad, but hopeful nonetheless.

"So, what's your story Mr. Billy?" she asked him, puffing out the smoke in Os.

"My story?"

"You went to Vietnam, didn't you?"

"How can you tell?"

"I can see it in your eyes," she said, squinting at him.

He didn't doubt that it wasn't just a guess (an educated one, considering the time), that she could see his eyes were dulled from having seen too much of what humans are not meant to see.

"My older brother went," she said. "He didn't make it back."

"I'm sorry."

"Not your fault."

He took a long drag, and she did the same.

"I bet making it back isn't easy either," she said, tapping the ash off the end of her cigarette.

"I went to Europe for a while, to get away."

"Did it help?"

He shrugged. "I saw the Eiffel Tower."

61

"Was it amazing?" she asked, sounding so naïve and easily impressed.

"That's just it—it wasn't. I'd seen it in pictures, you know. It was just like in the pictures. I'm starting to wonder if I'll always be disappointed."

"That's sad."

Her eyes were watery, like she was going to cry for him right then and there. That sadness, on his behalf, caught him off guard. He'd had this notion that life was simply a battle of clichés, thought that humans had become too desensitized to ever feel anything real, to ever be truly surprised and awed. She disproved this theory.

They took their last drags.

"Are you busy after the show?" he asked.

"That depends. Are you taking me somewhere?"

She rode in the passenger's seat of his Camaro, arm hanging out the window, making waves in the air.

"I'm not going to sleep with you," she said as he parallel parked outside his apartment building. "I'm not even going to kiss you."

"Okay," he said with a shrug, trying to make it seem like he wouldn't think of such a thing, though he'd already undressed her in his mind, ran his fingers along her sides, kissed her breasts, intertwined his limbs with hers.

"I think I want you to respect me. I think you're somebody

I'd want to keep around a while."

"Like how long?"

"A while."

They sat Indian-style on the olive-green shag carpet of his bedroom and listened to Bob Dylan and Miles Davis and John Coltrane, passing a joint back and forth until there was nothing left.

"You're like a Neil Young song," he said. "Soothing, mellow, calm."

"You're high."

"I'm serious. You walk with this slight lean backward, weight on your heels, like you have faith in the world that you just shouldn't have."

"Billy, you're really high," she said, laughing.

She sat next to him, humming along to "Tangled Up in Blue." He watched her lips twitch as she hummed, found himself unable to take his eyes off those lips. She caught his stare and smiled then leaned in and kissed him quickly. Then she went back to humming.

"Did you decide against keeping me around for a while?" he asked after the song ended.

"No, I still want to keep you around," she said. "Is that okay?"

"Sure, but what about me respecting you?"

"I can tell you already do because you didn't seem upset

when I said I wouldn't sleep with you."

"Are *you* high?" he said.

She turned to him again, touched her nose to his, and kissed him, longer this time. He opened his eyes, just for a moment, long enough to see that her eyes were closed, that she was losing herself in him. She pulled back, put her index finger to his mouth, and said, "I'm just doing my best not to disappoint you."

They fell in love fast, the way people did in those days. He became enamored with the little things—the way she jerked during bad dreams in the middle of the night, the way she swept her long hair up into a bun, always twisting the hair counterclockwise, the way she drove with her hands at six o'clock. Both of 'em. He was a ten-and-two kind of guy and decided she was his antidote.

After a year or so of loving her, he said he'd stopped searching for his heart of gold (quoting a Neil Young song) because he'd found it, and he asked her to marry him. She said yes. He knew she would because, like he'd told her that first night in his bedroom, she had faith.

Bill never thought much about fatherhood, but he knew that marrying Wendy would demand thinking about it. Wendy wanted kids, had dreams of children swinging from her arms like monkeys from a branch. She talked about the future family outings she envisioned—baseball games, the zoo, picnics at the beach. They made predictions for their first child's facial features: Wendy guessed it would have her mouth, his nose, and her eyes; Bill guessed it would have her mouth (including the gap in the teeth), her nose, and her eyes. Wendy said, "So you don't think it's going to look like you at all?" He smiled and said, "We can only hope."

When they'd been married a few years and Bill found a job with the Department of Water and Power, they decided it was time for baby to make three. They bought books of names, talked about Hannah or Molly if it was a girl, Zachary or Ethan if it was a boy. When they moved into their new house in the Hollywood Hills, they kept one bedroom empty, reserved for their future child.

A year passed; the room remained empty. Wendy put a rocking chair in the corner. Bill often found her sitting in it, rocking back and forth, staring intensely at a spot on the wall, as if their baby was lost somewhere in the plaster.

"Maybe we should see a doctor," he said, desperate not necessarily for a child but to have his wife back, hopeful eyes and all.

"No," she said, not looking at him.

She had lost her faith, grown depressed and distant, turned away from him and in on herself like a balled-up sock.

"Why not?"

"I don't want to know. If it's a problem with me, I'll hate myself."

"What if it's a problem with *me*?" he said.

"It's not."

She seemed so sure, which wasn't logical. He decided then that nothing is more frustrating, as a man, than a woman's refusal of his attempts to fix things.

"What about adoption?" he said. "We could always adopt."

"I don't think I could look at a child and not regret that it wasn't my own," she said. "It wouldn't be fair."

"Well, there must be something we can do. Let's see a doctor," he said, approaching the rocking chair. She looked at him, her stare hard and steely, then sighed.

"Don't you get it? It's not meant to be. It's just not."

He feared then that she was talking about their whole marriage.

A few days later, Bill came home from work and saw that Wendy had turned the should-have-been-nursery into a guest room, complete with a daybed and a nightstand with a digital clock. They didn't talk about it. He asked her if she was okay, and she said, "I think I'll paint the room a rose color, to match the bedspread." She'd given up.

They got a cat, Roxy, who became that something they needed to bind them together, something to be invested in, something to care about beyond themselves—a replacement child. Wendy went back to school to get a nursing degree then got a job in Labor and Delivery at Cedars-Sinai. Bill thought it would be hard for her, to be around the babies. But it seemed to be what she needed. Even after her shifts ended, she would sit with the newborns while their exhausted mothers slept. She had a shoebox full of thank-you cards those new mothers had sent her.

Roxy lived to be sixteen. When they put her to sleep, Wendy was heartbroken, called in sick to work for a week straight. He decided they needed a new Roxy. But, maybe a dog this time. He went to a breeder in Calabasas. There was one puppy left—the runt. He knew Wendy would appreciate that.

He went home, lit incense, set "Heart of Gold" on the record player, put the dog in a cardboard box by the door, and waited for Wendy.

He planned to make a speech when she walked through the door, about how he knew they could never replace Roxy but he wanted to see his wife happy again. He planned to open the box and present the puppy to Wendy. But, of course, the puppy did not comply with these plans. The moment Wendy walked in the door, the puppy leaped from the box, so excited she peed all over the carpet.

"Surprise," Bill said with a chuckle.

Wendy gasped. "She's ours?"

It was only when he confirmed this that Wendy took the dog in her arms, holding her like a baby, cradling her head.

"What'll we call her?" she asked Bill.

"Zuma," he said.

It was the name of their favorite Neil Young album.

Bill climbs into bed next to his wife with her freshly dyed hair.

"Wendy, you awake?"

"No," she says.

"Look, I'm sorry."

"I said I wasn't awake." She rolls away from him. "Put Zuma outside before you go to bed. It's hot. She'll want to swim."

"*I wish I could talk to you, you could talk to me, you know, like in the days that used to be,*" he says, butchering a Neil Young song, doing his best impression, his cracking, strained voice sounding more like that of aging Bob Dylan.

"I'm sleeping. Let Zuma outside."

He sighs and climbs out of bed, opens the door for the dog. Zuma lifts her head, walks toward him on her weak, failing legs. He follows her outside, watches her lower herself into the pool and swim to the ledge, the moonlight shining on the water. He crouches down and pets the dog's wet fur then tugs at his ring once again. It slips right off. He puts it in his sock and stares at his naked finger, the skin white and raw where the ring used to be. Zuma lingers on the step, working up the energy to get out of the pool. She used to just leap right out.

Bill goes to sleep that night without his ring on, just to see if it feels different, free.

He wakes up to Wendy shaking him. The early morning sun is coming through the blinds.

"Bill, get up, Bill," she says.

"What the hell is it?"

"It's Zuma," she says, her sleepy eyes scared, glossy.

He sits up and looks to Zuma's dog bed, expecting to see her there. But her bed, its lining like the inside of an old and worn UGG boot, is empty except for a red rubber bone. Wendy is already outside, standing by the pool.

"What is it?" he asks, approaching behind her.

She holds her hand to her mouth, tears primed on the ridges of her eyes. She points to the shallow end, where Zuma lays at the bottom, just still in the water, fur especially downy and soft, an expression of peace immortalized on her face. She looks like something preserved in a jar of formaldehyde in a chemistry lab.

"Oh, shit," he says.

She turns around and buries her head in his chest, sobbing.

"It must have happened during the night, right? Oh god, Bill. Do you think she suffered? Probably not, right? I mean, she looks happy. And look at her paws. She's in swimming position. Do you think she had a heart attack or something while she was swimming?"

He strokes her hair as her chest heaves up and down against his, her eyes wetting his shoulder.

"I'm sure that's what happened," he says.

"Really? You're sure? It was instant, right?"

"I'm sure," he says.

He goes to the shed to get the net they use to fish out leaves and twigs. He uses the pole attached to the net to push Zuma over to the steps, where Wendy is waiting, her pajama pants rolled up to her knees. He joins her on the steps, still wearing his socks. She takes Zuma's head, he takes her back legs, and they lift her out onto a white sheet, the one they've been laying on top of the rug Zuma liked to sleep on in their living room. It's covered with bloodstains from the sore on her back. They fold the sheet over her and stare.

"Can we bury her in the backyard?" Wendy asks.

"I'll dig a hole by the rose garden."

Using the pickax and a shovel, Bill digs her grave, good and deep. The beads of sweat accumulate in the wrinkles of his face, despite the cool chill of the morning air. While Wendy is inside, he puts Zuma in a wheelbarrow and rolls her to the grave. He lays her into the ground, picks a rose and places it on her body.

Wendy comes out, arms full of Zuma's favorite toys—a Snoopy stuffed animal with the plastic eyes missing, a tug rope, a tennis ball worn and slobbered on over the years. She brings out the jar of dog biscuits too.

"She was a good dog," Wendy says as they stand over the hole, looking down at their baby, surrounded by toys and biscuits.

"Yeah," Bill says, face reddening, tears coming unexpectedly. He buried a man in Vietnam and didn't cry then.

Wendy takes his hand, her thumb massaging the ravines

between his fingers. He's forgotten how comforting her grip is.

"Would it be bad to say I'm kind of relieved?" she whispers.

"It was her time," he says.

"She was suffering so long. She's free now, right?"

"Yeah," he says. "Free."

She puts her hand underneath his shirt and traces his spine with her fingertips. Chills follow her touch.

"Just you and me now," she says, kneeling down, pressing two fingers to her lips, then to the ground. *"Like in the days that used to be."*

He smiles as she stands and wraps her arms around him from behind. He realizes all over again that his shoulder is at the perfect height for her to rest her chin. She kisses his cheek softly.

"I'll be inside," she says.

He watches her walk away, her pajama pants still rolled up to her knees, the left leg slowly unrolling.

He covers Zuma with the soil, throws rocks on top just in case the coyotes come down from the hills. Then he reaches into his soggy sock for his ring, rolls it around in his palm, and slides it onto his finger. It goes right back on, right over his knuckle, easily.

thinking twice

SHE DIDN'T KNOW what had become of Adam Boyd. If she was honest with herself, he was the reason she'd come.

They gave her a name tag and a shove in the direction of the open bar—a reminder of who she was twenty years ago, and access to the liquid courage needed to admit who she'd become.

She stood against the wall, sipping a rum and Coke. People walked by, squinted to read her name tag, glanced at her face, and kept walking. It's not that she looked especially different from the girl in the Oceanside High 1976 yearbook; it's just that she'd come alone, and, in high school, she was always the girl known in relation to someone else—girlfriend of Adam Boyd, best friend of Chrissy Wallace.

Chrissy Wallace had died in a freak waterskiing accident just a few months before the reunion. There were a few whispers about it circling the bar.

"Is that who I think it is?" a voice called out.

She turned to see her past coming right toward her, looking strange in a suit and tie.

Adam Boyd.

He looked older, which surprised her, though it shouldn't have. So many years had passed and, yet, she still preserved him in her mind as sixteen, with worn sneakers and shaggy hair. She hadn't seen him since the summer before senior year, when his father, a sergeant general in the Marine Corps, got orders for their family to move to Virginia. When he left, he took her naïveté and virginity with him.

"Adam?" she said to him.

His hair was shellacked in an I-have-a-corporate-job sort of way. Wrinkles fanned out around his eyes and mouth, suggesting he'd smiled for many women other than her.

"Wendy? It's really you?"

"It sure is," she said, embarrassed of the smallness of her voice. She sounded so much like the girl she'd left behind.

"Wow. Wendy Quinby," he said, marveling.

"It's Wendy Addison now," she said.

He raised his eyebrows and said, "Lucky guy."

When she felt herself blush, she looked down so he wouldn't see.

"I didn't know if you'd make it. I kind of hoped you would," he said.

She'd had a feeling he would come. He'd always lamented the family moves when he was a kid, spoke of a desperation for the roots most other kids took for granted.

"It was a last-minute decision," she said.

He enfolded her in his arms, and she felt that rush of teenage excitement, a rush that took her back to a time she'd stored away in the cluttered attic of her mind.

The first time Wendy saw Adam Boyd, he was leaning against the side of a Mayflower moving truck parked at the house directly across the street from hers. He nodded hello in her direction, and she gave a wave. The following Monday, he showed up in her English class and said, "Hey, I think you're my neighbor," and she said, "I think you're right."

In a matter of days, Adam became the popular kid. Wendy would figure out later that he was adept at being the new kid in school and had a history of making friends easily. It was a skill he'd acquired after years of being a military brat, moving place to place, having to form alliances with strangers quickly for the purposes of social survival. He charmed everyone with boisterous jokes and impeccable impressions of teachers. Those were his tried-and-true talents. Like a homeless person with a grocery cart full of invaluable trinkets, those were the things he carried with him. They were all he had.

Wendy instantly fell for the charm. She started spending every day across the street, sitting cross-legged with him in the tree house the previous family had left behind. It was a relief to have this convenient escape from her own house, a house that had the stale, musty air of grief ever since her older brother was killed in Vietnam.

"He was just nineteen," Wendy told Adam during one of their tree house chats.

She hadn't really talked to anyone about her brother's death. She felt comfortable with Adam because he understood the war, lamented its casualties. Her girlfriends were so oblivious.

Wendy's brother had sent letters home to their parents, detailing the atrocities he witnessed while he was there. Wendy wasn't supposed to read the letters, but she'd snuck out of her room in the middle of the night to do just that. Her parents kept them in a neat stack in the kitchen drawer, held together with a rubber band.

Her once-innocent, always-laughing brother wrote of seeing his first dead Vietcong (VC, he called them), an infantryman with his face blown off, flies feeding on what was left. He wrote of seeing his first dead American, a radio operator whose body was floating in a river, ropes still tied around his hands and feet, a bullet hole in the back of his head. He wrote of the mildew smell, tree lines floating like islands in the rice paddies, horizontal rain, elephant grass, banana trees with their big plastic-looking leaves. He wrote of hacking through the jungle, wearing a poncho, head hooded and bowed, mud sucking at his boots. He wrote of malaria and blackwater fever and dysentery—more enemies. He wrote of his friend, a rifleman, who cried when he had to shoot a VC holding a baby. As a punishment for his tears, he was put on corpse duty, throwing bodies into a truck, to "toughen him up." He wrote about how they couldn't trust anyone on the other side, even the kids. *You look at them, in their eyes, and you see they hate you and they don't even know you. They've been raised to hate you. Even the natives who trade you canteens full of fresh water for C rations and cigarettes, they hate you. Even the girls who sell the Cokes, they hate you. So you hate them because you have to, to survive. Hell, one of our guys even shot a water buffalo, said it was a VC water buffalo. I guess you can't try to see goodness in anything here. You wander into jungles and get shot by snipers when you do that. You step into booby traps when you trust too much. That's what they tell us. You've got to see the worst in people to stay alive.*

In the end, it was a booby trap that got him. Wendy comforted herself with the thought that he just hadn't learned to see the worst in people. He'd died still believing in goodness.

"I miss him a lot," Wendy told Adam, the words catching in her throat. She drew hearts with her index finger in the dust of the tree house floor.

"Of course you do," he said. "That war was so stupid. My father and I had some big fights about it. If I'd been old enough, he would have wanted me to go over there. I'm sure of it. He probably would have been proud if I'd died."

"Don't say that."

"But it's true. The military is everything to him."

Adam couldn't wait to graduate high school, turn eighteen, and be free of his family. He was tired of all the moving, of telling people he was from "everywhere and nowhere." He fantasized of calling one place home. Oregon, he said. Or Colorado.

"How long do you think you'll be here?" Wendy asked him.

He shrugged. "Never know for sure. I'd be surprised if I graduated from Oceanside High."

When Wendy fell in love with him, she knew he was leaving. So she couldn't hate him when he did. Instead, she hated herself, for the shortsightedness of adolescence, for her teenage allegiance to all the usual clichés—living in the moment, throwing caution to the wind, getting swept away.

There were weeks of tree house talks before they kissed. That's the beautiful thing about first loves—they move at such a slow and deliberate pace. All relationships that follow can never compare, its participants just rushing past the hand-holding and tongue twisting and fondling in an attempt to recreate the intensity of that first love.

There were whispers at school about the couples who were having sex. Years later, Wendy still remembered the names—Julie and Brian, Carly and Mark, Samantha and

Donny. Wendy and Adam weren't on the list. There were whispers that Wendy was a "goody two-shoes."

It's not that she didn't want to. There were times when they were both naked, except for their underwear, in his twin bed and she'd say, "Let's just do it." He'd say, "Are you sure?" and she'd hesitate just long enough for him to say, "You're not sure yet." He didn't push it. He said he understood. "It's a big deal," he'd said. She'd agreed: "It is."

Then Adam's father got orders for the family to move across the country to Virginia. Suddenly, there was an urgency to their togetherness.

Wendy decided she was ready to lose her virginity the day after he'd given her the news that he was moving at the end of summer. He wasn't as upset about it as she was. He'd come to see all relationships as transitory, never let himself get too attached. When she'd cried, he'd said, confounded, "But I told you I would be leaving."

They sat in the tree house, passing away the July afternoon.

"I'm ready," she told him.

"For what?"

She raised her eyebrows at him suggestively. It took him a moment to understand. When he did, he smiled.

"Wendy," he said, making her name a complete sentence.

"Yes?"

"You're just saying that because I'm moving in a month."

"Maybe. Who cares? I want to."

"It won't change anything," he said. She thought she saw sadness in his eyes, but maybe it was pity.

"I know that," Wendy said.

But that was a lie. Secretly, she hoped it would change everything.

🌰

They planned it for when Adam's parents were out of town, scouting houses in Virginia. Their trip gave Wendy and Adam the rare opportunity to spend the night together, to pretend they were grown-ups. Wendy told her parents she was spending the night at Chrissy's house. They didn't care enough to question. Since her brother had died, they'd seemed to have given up on parenting entirely, concluding that it didn't matter how well you raised your children because the world those children entered was unfair. Tragedies were indiscriminate.

"You're really sure?" Adam asked her as they lay naked, him on top of her, his lips on her neck. A Bob Dylan record played in the background, "Don't Think Twice, It's All Right" the eerily appropriate soundtrack to this moment.

"It would be pretty cruel of me to change my mind at this point," she said.

She felt his lips spread into a smile on her neck.

"Well, you're allowed to change your mind. If you want to."

"I don't want to."

He kept kissing her neck as his body moved against hers. And then he found his way inside and she gasped, tears welling up in the corners of her eyes.

"Are you okay?" he asked, easing back and forth into her.

"Yes," she said, though she wasn't sure she was. It hurt a little. Gradually, though, the pain turned to pleasure. Before she could understand this pleasure, he was groaning, sweat from his body making their skin adhere together. Then he stopped and collapsed on top of her, his arms falling to either side of her body.

"I'm sorry," he said.

"For what?"

"That wasn't good for you."

"It was," she said. A lie, the first of many she would tell men who wanted to hear that they'd pleased her. It wasn't until years later, after she'd married Billy, when she finally had the confidence to provide constructive criticism, to instruct.

He pressed himself up so he hovered over her, his eyes scanning hers.

"I love you," he said.

A part of her thought, hoped, that meant he would stay. They could run away together. To Oregon. Or Colorado. They didn't need to finish high school. They could get jobs and get by. It would be romantic. All the kids at school would talk about them. They would be legendary.

But no.

He left a month later. There wasn't even a formal goodbye. He'd told her he didn't want that, said it would be easier that way. Easier for him, he meant. He could vanish and start over somewhere new. She had to stay behind and remember what was.

She watched from the front window of her house as a moving van came and big, burly men hauled boxes out of Adam's house with alarming efficiency. His mother ushered him into the back of their station wagon, and then he was gone. He didn't even look across the street in her direction to give a wave. He had to know she was watching.

She missed two periods before she realized Adam had left her with more than a broken heart.

"Didn't he pull out?" Chrissy asked.

Chrissy had started having sex with her boyfriend right after she heard about Wendy losing her virginity. Adolescence is a race to lose all those things that keep you naïve, to shed innocence in the hopes of becoming the mature, sophisticated person you dream of being. Wendy didn't feel mature and sophisticated though; she felt lost.

"I thought he did," Wendy said.

Chrissy shook her head in disgust. "He probably didn't do it right."

It was a few years after *Roe v. Wade*. Women applauded their right to choose. But Wendy hated the choice. In a way, she wished she didn't have a choice. She daydreamed of writing a letter to Adam, of telling him about the baby. He would come back to her. They would be a family. Back before choice, this was a man's obligation.

"I'll find out what clinic Meredith Turner went to when she had her abortion," Chrissy said.

"Meredith had an abortion?"

Chrissy rolled her eyes. "I swear, when Adam was here, you two lived under a rock together."

She said this like it was a bad thing, when all Wendy wanted was to crawl back under that rock with him again.

"Maybe I should take some time to think about it?" Wendy said.

Chrissy looked confused. "Think about what?"

Wendy shrugged.

"You're not thinking of keeping it, are you? Are you crazy? We're still in high school. Women fought for your right to have a life without a baby."

Wendy knew she was supposed to care about those women who fought for her, but she couldn't find comfort in a political movement.

"You can't have a baby, Wendy," Chrissy said.

Wendy nodded, resigned. "I know," she said. "You're right."

If she had been a few years older, maybe she wouldn't have said this. Maybe she wouldn't have gone through with exercising her rights. Maybe she would be a mother.

Of course, Adam didn't know any of this. Adam, standing before her at the stupid reunion, had no idea that Wendy carried their baby for a few short months. He had no idea that her abortion left her with adhesions on her uterus, which her doctor identified when Wendy finally made an appointment to find out why she couldn't get pregnant after she and Bill had been trying and trying and trying. Asherman's syndrome, the doctor had said. Wendy was too ashamed to tell Bill. It made some kind of karmic sense that she would not have a family. She took a tiny life when she was a teenager; she didn't deserve a child.

"Wendy?" Adam said, bringing her back to the present, the reunion.

Wendy blinked. "What? Sorry."

"Strange to be back, huh?"

"Yes," she said. "Strange."

She didn't know why she'd come. Bill was surprised she'd opened the invitation. When he saw it stuck to the fridge, he'd said, "You're actually thinking of going to this?"

Back when they first met and discussed all the details of their pasts, she'd told him she'd hated high school. She didn't say much about Adam, wanting to believe he hadn't meant much to her. "I might go," she'd told Bill.

He'd said he'd go with her "for the free booze." But she'd told him she wanted to go alone. "Making peace with the ol' demons of adolescence?" he'd joked.

"Something like that," she'd said.

"How the hell have you been?" Adam asked.

The ice in her rum and Coke rattled against the glass. She was out of liquid courage.

"Good," she said. "You?"

"Can't complain. Did you hear about Chrissy, the waterskiing accident? Terrible." He shook his head in dismay.

"Yeah. Terrible."

"Did you still talk to her?"

She shook her head.

Chrissy had taken Wendy to her abortion appointment, had waited out front until Wendy emerged with a huge pad stuffed in her underwear. They went to get ice cream, just like Wendy and her mom used to do after doctor's appointments when Wendy was a kid. After that day, Wendy didn't talk to Chrissy the rest of the summer. It was awkward between them by the time senior year started. There was an unspoken agreement that their friendship was over, and that was that. Adam wasn't there for senior year, so he didn't know.

"Strange how you can be so close to someone in high school and just lose touch, isn't it?"

She stared at him. "Yes," she said. "Strange."

He winced. He must have heard the resentment in her voice, despite her attempts to hide it, to play the role of the cool former girlfriend without a care in the world.

"I wanted to call you," he said. "So many times."

Is this why she'd come? To hear that he'd cared about her? To satisfy some part of her ego that he'd bruised all those years ago when he'd left and so easily forgotten her? If that was the case, she was ashamed of herself, ashamed that the bruise he'd left was still yellow, unhealed.

"But you didn't," she said.

"I was just a kid."

Her cheeks burned. "So was I."

In the car on the way to the reunion, she'd imagined herself telling him everything. She'd even said it aloud: *You got me pregnant.* She'd imagined the shock on his face. She'd imagined feeling some sort of power over him with this revelation, some smug satisfaction. She'd imagined the anger leaving her body, a catharsis.

But standing there before him, with his corporate hair, she didn't have the nerve. Maybe it was because of the rum rolling through her veins. Or maybe she just realized that telling him would make it worse. He would care, momentarily. He would express a socially respectable amount of regret. But at the end of the night, after consuming as many drinks as necessary to endure this confrontation with his past, he would do what he'd been trained to do from an early age— leave and forget.

"So, tell me everything," he said with a tense laugh, trying to steer the conversation away from the resentment she had not been able to hide.

She was suddenly so tired. She didn't want to tell him

everything. She wanted to be home with Bill. She wanted to go to bed early, with Roxy, their cat, curled up on her chest.

"I think I'm going to go," she told Adam.

"Really? Already?" he said.

"Yeah." She held out her empty glass toward him, said, "Could you—"

He took the glass from her. "Sure, of course, yeah."

As she turned to leave, he called after her: "I'd still love to catch up sometime, if you want."

She looked at him as he fumbled in his pocket, retrieving a stack of business cards. He'd brought business cards. She didn't hate him anymore; she felt sorry for him, in a way.

"That's okay," she said, as if he was someone on a street corner offering her a coupon for window cleaning.

He looked disappointed, though she was sure he was secretly relieved. She started to walk away again.

"Wendy," he called.

She turned back, once more, and looked at him expectantly.

"I really am sorry," he said.

She gave him her most understanding smile and said, "Don't think twice, it's all right."

all the acorns
on the forest floor

"**I'VE BEEN WATCHING** it all day," Jake says when I come home from work.

"It" is the hummingbird nest, constructed in the tree outside the window above Jake's desk. "It" has become somewhat of an obsession.

Jake wanted to name the mother bird, so we chose Georgina, Georgie for short. For the past week, when we wake up in the morning, one of us goes to the window to report on her status: "Georgie's there!" We do the same before bed.

"No sign of her?"

He shakes his head, sullen. He worked from home today—a rarity—so he could keep watch. His eyes are wide with more distress than I've ever seen on his infamously stoic face.

The nest is so tiny, a compact cup made of bits of leaves and something that looks like cotton. It must have taken the mother several days to make it, several days of gathering materials from around our yard and weaving them together into a home for her future offspring. There is a level of meticulousness involved; that much is obvious.

We never saw the eggs. We just saw her sitting on the nest and assumed they were there, warmed by her. The internet said hummingbird nests usually have two. The internet also said that hummingbirds lay the smallest eggs of all birds— smaller than jelly beans. It was plausible that two jelly beans could fit in that tiny cup of a nest, but I couldn't imagine how hatched babies would have enough room.

We know they've hatched. We've used a stepladder to peek in. We've seen the little black bodies, pressed so close to each other that it was difficult at first to determine if there were one or two. There were two, evidenced by two tiny gold beaks.

Now that the mother has not returned to tend to them, we wonder if she saw us, if she thinks we are predators who either consumed or tainted her babies, if this is our fault.

"I think they're about two weeks old," Jake says. "They have stippling."

I've never heard this word—*stippling*. He's been googling.

He says it's been heartrending to watch them up close. Every half hour, their skinny, ill-supported necks emerge from the nest, their beaks open. They need food. He went to the pet store and bought some nectar. It's in what looks like a child's juice box. He emptied a bottle of Visine and put the nectar in there. He's been climbing up the ladder to place a few droplets in their open mouths.

"I don't know what else to do," he says.

I want to cry watching his agony. He will be a great father.

A few weeks ago, I was at the gym—a family-run place where people know each other by name—when one of the trainers found an injured hummingbird on the outdoor running track. Something was wrong with its wing. She'd put the bird in the palm of her hand then into a shoebox. She'd gone online and found a hummingbird rescue nearby. "Who knew?" she'd said.

I tell Jake about the rescue, and we find the website. The rescue is run by one woman, Monique, out of her house. He emails Monique with the subject line "Abandoned babies." I tease him for being too dramatic, an attempt at comic relief.

She calls within a half hour. We are on our way to the park that overlooks the harbor. This is how we are celebrating our anniversary—a couple of pizzas from Agostino's and the sunset. We wanted to have a bonfire at the beach, but all the firepits were taken. When we got married on Memorial Day weekend last year, we didn't anticipate the crowds at our future anniversary celebrations.

Jake is driving, so I talk to her. "I'm Alex, Jake's wife," I say. "We think the babies are about two weeks old."

She says if that's the case, they are old enough to regulate their own temperature, so the mother does not have to sit on them. She says the mother is probably out getting food and that she comes by so quickly that Jake has missed seeing her. I know Jake, though. I know that when he says he's been watching, he's been *watching*. He is intense that way. He marches to the top of Mount Whitney without stopping. He wakes up some days and decides to embark on one-hundred-mile bike rides. I've joked that he should start an adventure company called On a Whim and a Prayer.

"I mean, we're not sure of the age. We're guessing," I say. "Maybe they're younger."

This frustrates her. "If they were younger and without their mom for as long as you say, they wouldn't be alive."

She is talking to me like I'm an idiot.

"Are their eyes open?" she asks.

"No," I say.

She huffs. "Then they are not two weeks old. You need to give me more accurate information if I'm going to help you."

I want to cry. It's the hormones, I guess. They are coursing through my body, though I feel relatively normal now that the phase of constant queasiness has passed.

"Send me a picture," she says.

I tell her we are out, that we will hope to be home before it's dark so we can get a good photo. There is judgment in her voice, asking how we can possibly be "out" with this potentially life-threatening situation in our backyard. She doesn't know it's our anniversary.

It feels like gas bubbles when the baby moves. It's very sporadic, much to my chagrin. I keep thinking that if I concentrate hard enough, I can mentally connect with our unborn daughter and tell her to move in a way that reassures me she's alive. But that's not the case. Our daughter is already her own person; she moves when she wants.

We have a name for her, but I struggle to use it. Jake doesn't. I suppose I'm too afraid to get attached to her, only to lose her the way we lost her brother—Ben, our son who wasn't.

We email a photo of the birds to Monique before we go to bed. We don't expect her to respond quickly, so we go to sleep, telling each other that the morning will reveal whether the mother bird is truly gone. If she is, the babies will be dead. They wouldn't be able to survive the night.

The next morning, before using the bathroom or making coffee, Jake goes outside and climbs the ladder to the nest. I sit up in bed, waiting for his report.

"One of them is dead," he says.

I accept this fact quickly; I am good at receiving bad news now, a pro. "But one is alive?" I say. We, as humans, are conditioned for happiness. In the worst tragedies, we look for silver linings, bright sides.

"One is alive," he confirms.

He checks his email and there is a message from Monique, sent after we fell asleep.

"If the photos are current, those birds are very young. The mother should be sitting on them. Something must have happened to her. You need to bring them inside."

We feel guilty now, like we are responsible for the death of the one baby.

Jake uses a pair of scissors to cut the branch from the tree and bring the nest inside. I plug in my heating pad on the kitchen counter, the heating pad I'd used to "warm my uterus" when we were trying to get pregnant. I thought warmth would encourage the embryo to implant and grow. Perhaps I was right.

Jake places the nest on the warm heating pad. He manages a few drops of nectar down the baby's gullet, but then he—we call the bird a "he"—stops opening his beak.

Jake calls Monique. She says we should bring the survivor to her. She says to give her twenty minutes; she needs to make herself decent.

"Is there any chance of survival here?" Jake asks her.

"This is a difficult one," she says. "That bird is very young."

I marked each Saturday in my day planner with Ben's age—eight weeks, nine weeks, ten weeks. On those Saturdays, I made an event of looking up "this week in your pregnancy" information online. "This week, the baby has paddles that will become arms." "This week, the digestive tract and reproductive organs are forming." "This week, the eyelids and eyebrows have developed." I reported these things to Jake.

The websites always compare the baby's size to food: a poppy seed, then a peppercorn, then a pomegranate seed, then a blueberry, then an olive, then a cherry, then a kumquat, then a brussels sprout, then a passion fruit. It was around the time he was the size of a passion fruit that we saw him on ultrasound, his arms waving and legs kicking as he floated in the black sea of amniotic fluid that was his home. I went out and bought him his first outfits—nautical-themed onesies, a Dodgers baseball T-shirt. In retrospect, as irrational as this may be, I wonder if this jinxed us.

At sixteen weeks, I invited my mom to our ultrasound appointment. "He was dancing around on-screen last time," I told her.

This time, though, he wasn't moving. We stared. The black sea of amniotic fluid was gone. There were just small pockets of black now, the baby squished between them. He was tucked in on himself, contorted. It was difficult to know what we were looking at. His heart rate was fine, but he was measuring small. Without the space provided by the fluid, he couldn't stretch and grow.

The doctor told us it could be a deformity with the kidneys or urinary tract, meaning Ben was swallowing the amniotic fluid but not processing and excreting it properly. He also said it could be a problem with the placenta. He told me to rest and come back in two weeks. When we asked what would happen if the fluid levels did not improve, he told us the baby would become more constrained and would likely press against the umbilical cord, reducing blood flow and causing . . . He didn't say it outright, but we knew what he meant. *Death.*

He gave us a printout of the ultrasound image. Jake wouldn't look at it, and I couldn't blame him. Ben looked like an alien, his head turned toward us, the black circles of his eyes seemingly saying, "Help! I'm in trouble." This image gave me nightmares for months.

I bought a fetal Doppler online so I could check to make sure Ben was alive. I lay in bed, squeezed gel on my belly, and moved the wand around. There it was—a strong heart rate of 159, like a muffled recording of a horse galloping. The next day, I tried for hours and couldn't get a reading.

"Let me try," Jake said. He didn't have any luck either.

"We're probably not doing it right," I said. "The baby is so small and changes position all the time." This is what women on the online message boards said. I wanted to believe them.

At our follow-up appointment, the doctor asked me the usual questions about how I was feeling. He tricked us into thinking this was just a normal appointment. But then he moved the transducer over my belly, sighed, and said:

"I'm not seeing a heartbeat."

It was April Fools' Day. For a brief second, I thought, hoped, he was playing a demented joke on us.

The doctor kept moving the transducer around my belly, investigating. I hated the medical interest on his face, the intrigue.

"Can you stop?" I screamed.

He stopped. Jake clutched my ankle, held on to it like it was a railing in a fast-moving subway car.

Ben was the size of a bell pepper.

There were two choices: they could induce labor so I could give birth to Ben and see him, or I could have surgery, a D&E. I didn't want to see Ben as a lifeless, gray, very miniature human. When I told Jake I wanted to do the surgery, relief spread across his face.

The diagnosis on my surgery packet: fetal demise. I can't imagine a more depressing pair of words. When I woke up after the procedure, I was crying—either because of pain or because I knew, even in my unconscious state, that they were taking our baby.

In the days that followed, my breasts were engorged and sore because my body thought I'd given birth and needed to feed the baby. My belly was a pooch of failure, its protrusion reminding me of what I'd lost. I couldn't sleep, even with the sleeping pills prescribed to me. It was like I was wired to listen for a crying baby who wasn't there.

The mornings were the hardest. I'd wake up thinking it was just a nightmare and, when my psyche refused to exit denial, I had to relive the whole ordeal.

I'm not seeing a heartbeat.

Jake couldn't be around me. While I sobbed and bled, he left the house, spent twelve-hour days at work. On one of those first nights without Ben, he went to a hockey game with his sister's husband. I hated him at the time. I hated that he couldn't sit next to me and put his hand on my shoulder. I hated that he couldn't cry with me. He busied himself with too many tasks—going on long runs, scrubbing the cement in the backyard, volunteering to collect signatures for local causes that had never mattered to him before. This was how he dealt with his parents' diagnoses too—his father's ALS, his mother's cancer. I remember thinking, on our visit to Jake's wheelchair-bound father, that his parents might get to meet their grandchild. The only obstacle was their survival; I didn't even think about the baby's.

The doctors gave us no explanation for Ben's death. "These things happen," they'd said. That wasn't good enough for me. I had to blame someone. I chose Jake's father.

"It's the gene," I told Jake.

I became convinced Ben had died because he'd inherited the defective gene, the ALS gene that was killing Jake's father and would possibly kill Jake. It's not that the gene itself would kill a fetus; the disease would take fifty years to show itself. I knew that. But I'd created a story in which Ben had died because God wanted to spare him a future with this horrid disease. I'd never really believed in God, but I had to for my story to make any sense.

"Alex," Jake said, taking my arm, trying so hard to be patient with my insanity. "It's not the gene."

To prove it, he got tested. He didn't tell me he was doing it. He just texted one day: "I'm negative."

I didn't know what he meant. My first thought: *No, you're not. You are the most positive person I know.*

He called me to explain. "I'm negative. I don't have the gene. Ben couldn't have had the gene."

I was relieved, of course. But that anger at his father had given me some life, in a strange way. Without it, I was like a deflated balloon.

I sit with the heating pad and the nest in my lap as the robotic voice on my phone directs us to Monique's home off Ortega Highway. We decided to leave the dead baby with its sibling. For warmth, we said. But, really, I think we couldn't bear to dispose of it. We would leave that task to Monique, the professional.

When we turn onto her street, it's easy to guess which house is hers. The front yard is overgrown with bushes of flowers, an idyllic feeding ground for the birds she loves enough to save. Jake parks the car and comes around to open my door. As we walk up the steps, we hear a woman's voice inside.

"Do you think she's talking to another human or to all her birds?" I say.

Jake manages a laugh.

She opens the door. I had expected someone with dyed red hair and a flowy dress and bare feet, someone with crystals hanging around her neck. But Monique is just an average fifty-something woman with slightly frizzy brown hair and a round, kind face. On the car ride over, we'd wondered aloud if she would have hummingbird figurines in her house, if her passion extended to other birds like parakeets and parrots. She doesn't invite us in, though. She pulls the door shut behind her, joins us on the porch. This is her home, after all. She doesn't know who we are. We could be as strange as we assume she is.

A clipboard rests on her forearm. We trade items—she gives me the clipboard and I give her the nest. While I fill out the intake form with details of the bird's life as we know it, she pets the living baby with more force than I thought his small body could handle. There is no apprehension in her touch. She makes sure the other one is, in fact, dead and says, "What a shame." I swallow hard.

"This is baby season," she says. "I have eight of them right now."

"Eight? Wow," I say.

I wonder if she can ever go on vacation, if she can ever leave her house at all. Maybe she is like me, happy to have an excuse to decline social invitations, disinterested in elaborate out-of-town trips. Maybe she likes the purpose that comes with feeding baby birds every half hour.

"It's hard to get the babies, but it's even harder when someone brings an injured female adult," she says, shaking her head. "I just know she has a nest somewhere, you know? I know those baby birds will die without her. I tell the people to look for the nest in the area they found the bird, but the nests . . . they're so small."

I tell her that this one, this nest, was right outside our window, as if the mother placed it there, as if she knew she would abandon her babies and wanted to ensure someone would help them, like a teenager leaving her newborn in a basket in a hospital lobby.

"Something must have happened to the mother," she says.

According to the internet, hummingbirds get in fights. They are one of the most aggressive birds, despite their size. They will attack crows, even hawks, who infringe on their territory. They are easily injured.

"Do you think this one has a chance?" Jake asks her.

She sighs, still petting the small body, coaxing the baby to stretch his weak neck upward.

"It's hard to say. Even in the best of circumstances, only about half of hummingbirds make it to maturity."

After we lost Ben, one of the nurses said, in an attempt at comfort, "You'll just have to try again. One will stick."

I still remember how she flicked her wrist dismissively. Dina was her name, the nurse. For a while, Jake and I would get a laugh out of each other by saying, "Remember Fucking Dina?"

She had this line, something that sounded stolen from a pamphlet on pregnancy loss:

"Nature is very wasteful," Fucking Dina had said. "Just look at all the acorns on the forest floor."

I will always envy women who pee on a stick and throw a nine-month-long celebration party, women whose greatest worry is weight gain and what color to paint the nursery, women who post their ultrasound photos on Facebook with reckless abandon. I will never be one of them.

I didn't even take a picture of the pregnancy test this time. I did everything possible to keep hope at a comfortable distance, thinking if I hoped less, the pain of loss would be less, thinking I could have some control over my possible heartache.

I decided against early blood testing that would confirm the embryo's viability—the numbers have to double every couple days; if they don't, the baby never had a chance. *Just look at all the acorns on the forest floor*. I didn't want the stress of the testing, the waiting for the results, the near-panic attack when the phone number of the doctor's office flashed on my screen. We decided to hold our collective breath and wait for our first ultrasound appointment. There would either be a heartbeat or there wouldn't. I didn't bother googling about every twinge. I pretended to be emotionless. I pretended to be Jake.

Jake's parents died shortly after we got married, within two months of each other. He didn't cry. Instead, he started training for a marathon. This is his way.

When we found out I was pregnant, he signed up for a city-sponsored disaster planning course and started watching shows like *Doomsday Preppers*, about families preparing for the apocalypse. Once, he left his laptop on the kitchen table and went to the bathroom, so I peeked to see what had his attention. On his screen was a web page with the headline "Can you drink pool water in an emergency?" Every Thursday, for three hours, he learned about fire safety and disaster psychology and medical operations and search-and-rescue and CPR and terrorism. He wanted to be ready—for the worst.

There was a heartbeat at our first ultrasound appointment. I was light-headed, dizzy, nearly fell off the table as the doctor pointed to the flicker on the screen. We'd chosen a new doctor because I couldn't bear the sight of the one who'd said, "I'm not seeing a heartbeat." In his office, he reviewed the basics of pregnancy, and I nodded, though I wasn't listening. My ears were ringing. The stress of it all would give me a migraine the rest of the day.

Most people would say, "We're having a girl!" I shudder at the arrogance of those words. When we started telling select loved ones, we simply said, "It's a girl." We didn't know if we'd be lucky enough to *have* her. I've kept a list of the people who know about the pregnancy so I don't have to rack my brain to remember who to tell if something goes wrong. The day after they took Ben from me, I delegated that task to Jake, desperate to avoid a clueless friend texting to ask, "How's the mama-to-be?"

Jake started my maternity wardrobe for me when I complained I couldn't button my pants. He went to an expensive boutique in North County, left the shopping bag for me on our bed, the receipt sticking out the top. A sweater, two pairs of pants, a loose-fitting shirt, and a quintessential pregnant-woman shirt with the ruching on the side to allow for belly expansion. I was afraid to try on the clothes, to admit to the world that I was a pregnant woman, a woman with something to lose. I did, though. Everything fit except one pair of pants. Jake was brave for trying; pants are never easy for me.

When I went to return them, the clerk said, "Sorry, we only do store credit." So, I picked out a shirt. I still had twenty dollars to spend. The only items that price were baby clothes. I pawed through them, telling myself not to "ooh" and "aah," even in the privacy of my own mind. I'd told Jake I didn't want to buy anything for the baby, didn't want to tempt fate that way. But the store credit forced me to confront my illogical superstitions. I bought a pair of newborn pajamas with kitty cats on them. The clerk asked if I wanted to add my name to their contact list. I declined, thinking that if I lost the baby, I didn't want to keep getting emails about discounts on breastfeeding-friendly blouses. When I came home, I gave Jake my guiltiest look and said, "I did a bad thing," pulling the pajamas from the bag, revealing the potential jinx.

There are moments I ask him, "Am I really pregnant?" There are moments I wonder if I'm so grief-stricken over Ben that I'm delusional, that I'm imaging this. I have dreams that I've lost the baby. I have dreams of waking up in a pool of blood, the loss all over the sheets. The other day, some coworkers at the library were talking about whether they dream in color or in black and white; recalling my nightmares, I said, "In color."

Nearly every morning, it takes me a moment to orient myself, to confirm our reality. I step on the scale daily, not because I care how many pounds I am gaining, but because the weight assures me that our daughter is really inside.

I've started writing letters to her, our daughter, in an attempt to connect with her, after all these weeks of attempting not to connect with her. I don't tell anyone about these letters, want them to be between me and her. If we lose her, only she will know how I got attached to her when I should have known better. *Fool me once, shame on you. Fool me twice . . .*

A patron at the library touched my belly last week. "Look at you!" she'd said. She's a regular, but still, I don't *know* her. I felt assaulted, exposed. There is no hiding now. My secret is no longer safe. I am on display for all to see, a public marvel.

Is this your first? People keep asking that, and I don't know how to answer. If I say yes, I am denying the existence of Ben. If I say no, I have to explain. Sometimes I say, "My first that's made it this far," which usually elicits confusion.

People say they are "so excited" for us. I can't match their enthusiasm. I force a smile. I refrain from lecturing them on all the things that can still go wrong. Placental abruption. Umbilical cord strangling. Listeria. Toxoplasmosis. Cervical incompetence. Premature labor. Unexplained stillbirth. Don't they know? How do they speak with such confidence about the baby's arrival? How is it possible they think I am constructing a nursery?

I thought my disdain of pregnant women would vanish by this point, but it has not. I can't relate to them—their discussions of swollen feet, their obsession with baby clothes, their photos of their growing bellies, their "babymoons," their baby showers (and "sprinkles" for second and third and fourth children) where they smash chocolate bars in diapers and guess belly circumference for fun and prizes. How can they make light of something so serious? The bliss of their ignorance is exasperating.

Friends have started asking about my baby shower. They think I'm being coy when I say I don't want one, but just the thought of accumulating all those things—the clothes, the toys, the gadgets—before she's even here makes my heart race. "You'll change your mind," they say. They assume I'll relax, that my worrying will abate.

I made the mistake of assuming this as well. I told myself, "I'll relax when I hear the heartbeat," then "When I get past the first trimester," then "When the genetic screening tests come back," then "When the anatomy scan is normal," then "When she's bigger than a bell pepper," then "When I feel her move." I've come to accept that I'll never be at ease. I've come to accept that this is motherhood.

Monique emails to say that the baby bird is doing well. He's warm, and he's eating. She uses the word miracle. I wonder if she's surprised when Jake keeps contacting her, asking for updates. The most recent: "His eyes are open now."

We fly to Indiana for Jake's cousin's wedding. I worry about germs on the plane. I worry about straying from my superfoods diet. I worry about taking all my vitamins. I worry about finding a half hour to take a walk every day. I worry about having trouble sleeping; I always do when I'm away from home.

His family is surprised to see my pregnant belly. "We didn't know," they say. Of course they didn't. My grandmother still doesn't know. During the father-of-the-bride speech, his uncle mentions that he's been fighting a cold. So when he leans in to congratulate me on the baby, I hold my breath as long as I can.

When we come home, I ask if Jake's heard from Monique. He says he hasn't.

"It's hard not to think about the one that died," he says.

"Yeah, I know."

I keep thinking about the mother. I hope she didn't come back to find her babies gone. In a way, I hope she died.

"We should ask if she does visiting hours," he says.

"We can show up with a Get Well Soon balloon," I joke. He rolls his eyes, and I realize he's serious.

He emails her. I wonder if he'll blame my hormones, my sentimentality, for this strange request.

Just twenty minutes later, his phone rings and he says, "It's her." He puts the call on speaker so I can hear.

"Hi, Monique," we say in unison.

"Well, hello there," she says.

"You got my email then?" he says.

"I did. And I'm sorry to tell you, but our little bird is gone."

My heart plummets to my feet, and I kneel instinctively, as if to pick it up off the floor.

"Gone?" Jake says. His voice cracks in a way it rarely does. He has a deep, strong voice, a reliable radio voice, a voice that doesn't falter.

"Oh," she says hurriedly, "not *gone* gone. To the aviary. He was ready to fly the coop."

The look on Jake's face is that of a child who has just won a goldfish at a county fair—excitement, awe.

"So he's doing well?" he says. He is desperate for confirmation. I place my hand on his, interlace my fingers with his, squeeze.

"As far as I know. I don't think he's going to check in with me. You know how teenagers are."

The three of us laugh. We thank her for saving him, and she says, "I just fed him and kept him warm. You saved him."

On Mother's Day, Jake surprised me with flowers and chocolate-covered strawberries, telling me with gestures instead of words that I am already a mother, even though I am reluctant to call myself that.

He is already a father; that I can admit. At the gym, he listens to books about the brain development of babies. "Did you know the baby has *dreams*?" he said the other day. He's already started calling day care centers. He's printed out all kinds of information from the internet—games to play with infants, how to make your own toys, recipes for baby food. He keeps all the papers in a binder.

Father's Day is today, and I have something for him.

"It's nothing big," I say. The box it arrived in is big, so I feel the need to say this.

He unwraps it. It takes him a moment to realize what it is. It's not a typical one—plastic and red. I wanted something nicer than that. This one is made from a glass antique bottle.

"A hummingbird feeder?" he says.

I nod.

"We can start our own rescue," he says.

"I'm not sure we'll have time for an official rescue when the baby arrives."

When. This may be the first time I have spoken of our daughter as if she will be here.

"I was thinking," he says. "We should move your reading chair into my office so we can start working on the nursery."

One luxury of our current childlessness is that we have our bedroom, an office, and a room for very occasional guests (and my reading chair). The guest room will become the nursery when the baby is here.

When.

Jake goes on: "This book I'm reading says you should be nesting."

"Nesting," I say.

This is something Jake does when he's unsure—repeat back what's just been said to him. If I suggest Chinese for dinner and he says "Chinese . . . ," that means he is not convinced Chinese is the best choice but he hasn't figured out what to offer instead.

"We can always move it back, if we need to," he says. "Let's just see how it looks. Just think—you'll have a view of the hummingbirds."

I can't help but think of the mother bird, of the tiny cup of a nest she constructed with such care, of the babies she abandoned—likely against her will. I can't help but think of her sorrow. If she is alive, she will go on to make another nest, to try again. Nature is as stubborn and persistent as it is wasteful.

"Okay," I say. Then again: "Okay."

the Craigslist baby

SHE APPROACHES THE nurses' station with the telltale grimace, holding her belly in her hands. She is alone, young, maybe just a teenager. Dina thinks she could be *the one*.

For the past several months, Dina's had this fantasy of stealing a baby. Not just any woman's baby—she's not some kind of sociopath—but the baby of a wayward youth. She would be doing the girl a favor.

"Dina, should I get a room ready?" Stacy asks.

Stacy's a new nurse, fresh out of school. Dina has worked the Labor and Delivery unit since she was Stacy's age. There's a lot of turnover on this unit, so after just ten years, she's considered the veteran, along with Wendy. The two mother hens who, ironically, are not mothers.

"Is this your first baby, hon?" Dina asks the girl, though she's sure it is. She can tell by the fear on the girl's face.

The girl nods through moans. When the contraction releases its grip on her, she says, "Last name's Delgado. First name's Alyssa. I preregistered."

This, the preregistration, shows that the girl is not as irresponsible as her belly suggests.

"Let me check her first," Dina says to Stacy.

The first-timers are always slow to progress. They come in convinced they're just moments away from a baby falling out of them. They can't fathom the pain could get any worse. Usually, they are hours away from actually delivering. Dina has the hard job of breaking that demoralizing news.

Dina walks the girl to a wheelchair, tells her to sit, then pushes her down the hallway to triage. It's a Wednesday, midmorning, not that busy. The triage room is empty for the time being.

"I'm going to need you to get up on the bed," Dina says. The girl's face contorts in the midst of another contraction. Sweat beads dot her forehead.

When the contraction passes, the girl sits on the bed then swings up her legs and lies flat. Women forget this about labor—that it offers breaks. The pain is not constant. Dina tries to tell women this as they scream and curse. "It's all temporary. It's going to be over soon." They are never consoled.

Dina inserts her gloved hand into the girl, assessing her cervix. Just as she suspected—she's dilated only one centimeter.

"Just one," she tells the girl.

"One what?" the girl says.

"Centimeter."

The girl does not seem to understand what this means. Clearly, she has not taken the birthing classes that most women take these days, creating an illusion of control over the mysterious horror that is about to befall them. Some women arrive with doulas and huge exercise balls and twinkly lights to hang in their rooms. Their birth plans state that the room should be dim and everyone should speak in soft voices. These women all want a natural birth. They want to labor in a tub while listening to Enya. Dina makes bets with the other nurses about which ones will request drugs. Most of them do. Dina's almost always right.

"Is one centimeter bad?" the girl says.

She has big, brown cow eyes, full of innocence. If you looked at just those eyes, you would never believe this girl had lost her virginity.

"It just means you have a ways to go," Dina says, squeezing the girl's hand.

The girl nods and grips Dina's hand, hard, as another contraction comes. Dina's hands are used to this. She has broken a finger only once.

"You're not going to send me home, are you?" the girl says, terror in her eyes.

"Depends. If you want an epidural, we can hook you up to that now. If you want to labor on your own, it's best to do that at home and come back when you're further along."

Women have cursed at Dina before upon receiving this news. *You want me to fucking go home?* That's what they say.

Recently, one woman said, "You must not have had a child before. If you had, you wouldn't be such a bitch." Dina just nodded and forced a smile. There was so much truth in that woman's statement: perhaps if she'd had a baby, she wouldn't be such a bitch.

"I want the epidural," the girl says. The look on her face says *Duh*, and Dina can't help but smile.

It's not that Dina doesn't *want* a child. She wishes she was one of those women who turn up their noses at basic biology and ignore all the social pressures to procreate—but she's not. She's wanted to be a mother since she was a child herself. She toted around Cabbage Patch dolls, rocking them in her arms and feeding them from pretend bottles. Her mother had said, "You've always had that maternal instinct." She didn't say it to be hurtful. She said it to imply that this is what makes Dina a good nurse. As if her nursing career, or any career for that matter, could fill the void left by childlessness.

She blames her childlessness on Derek, the man she dated for the better (or worse, in hindsight) part of nine years. After year one, her mother warned her that if he didn't propose, he wasn't serious. Milk for free and all that. She dismissed her mother, told her times were different now, couples lived together for years before saying those all-important vows. She should have listened. Three days before her thirty-sixth birthday, he ended it. He made it sound like he'd had some kind of epiphany, like he'd meditated under a tree and realized he didn't love her anymore. The reality was much simpler: he'd taken up with another nurse. Derek was a doctor, a cliché.

Dina met Garrett at a bar, of all places. They got married after only six months. A whirlwind romance, her mother said. Dina hated that word—*whirlwind*. It sounded so flippant and whimsical and doomed-for-failure. When they got engaged, she felt sheepish telling people. She'd always been the judgmental friend, asking questions like "Are you sure it's not too fast?" and "Are you sure it's love and not just lust?" Like she was the conservative bad cop columnist for *Cosmopolitan*. And there she was, marrying a guy she'd known half a year.

It wasn't a secret that she wanted a baby. Dina used to roll her eyes at women discussing their biological clocks, but then she felt her own tick-tick-ticking away. Garrett wanted a family too. He wasn't one of those men who needed convincing. Right after they got married—a small courthouse ceremony, followed by a lunch reception at their favorite Italian restaurant—they started trying. *Trying*. She'd come to hate that term, thought it sounded so desperate. Those first months, she was excited as the date of her period approached, convinced she would miss it and then pee on a stick and celebrate. But her period came with depressing regularity.

After about six months of this *trying* business, she went to see her gynecologist for her annual exam. While the doctor was peering between Dina's legs, Dina stared at the ceiling and confessed that she hadn't been able to get pregnant. The doctor lifted her head and said, "Why don't we do some tests to see how your eggs look?"

Dina remembered back to college, when she was just nineteen or twenty, and she responded to an ad offering ten thousand dollars for her eggs. She went through with it, gave herself injections of drugs that were supposed to increase her production. She wanted the money so she could move out of her parents' house once and for all. At the end of the whole thing, the doctor said he'd retrieved twenty-something eggs. He said that was very good. She'd felt strangely proud.

"I donated eggs in college," Dina told the doctor. "They said my eggs were great then."

The doctor gave her a smile that seemed amused at the time but, in retrospect, was slightly pitying.

"Well," the doctor said, "I'm guessing that was a while ago."

A week later, Dina got a phone call from the doctor.

"Your FSH is very high."

Dina thought that was a good thing. *High* is often a good thing. Now, she longs for those days of naïveté, when she didn't even know what FSH was. Follicle-stimulating hormone. The high number means her body is working hard to release an egg every month—*putting a foot on the gas pedal*, is what the doctor said, *to get things going*. The high number means she probably doesn't have many eggs left. And the ones she does have left may not be very good. *Scraping the bottom of the barrel*—that's the way the doctor put it.

"What does it mean for me, exactly?" Dina asked, unsure if she wanted to know.

"It's highly unlikely you'll get pregnant on your own," she said. "With numbers like yours, you're probably a couple years from menopause."

"*Menopause*?" Dina was startled by her own shriek. She was only thirty-eight. Menopause was for women in their fifties. Menopause was for grandmothers.

"It can happen early for some women," the doctor said.

Dina hated the doctor for her matter-of-factness. And she hated Derek, all those years wasted on someone who was just waiting for a better nurse to come along. She'd always thought she had time, assumed the universe was just waiting on her to decide to start a family: *Oh good, you're finally ready now? Great! Here's a baby.* Now it seemed that assumption was arrogant, foolish.

Garrett said they should keep trying.

"My mom had me when she was thirty-nine," he said.

Dina suddenly hated his mother. It was an irrational hate, the most potent kind. "Good for her and her eggs."

"I wasn't trying to—"

"Just stop," she told him.

They did keep trying. Trying to have a baby or trying to prove the doctor wrong, Dina didn't know anymore. She bought ovulation test strips that told her when her body was releasing a probably bad egg. They scheduled sex around that event. Literally, scheduled. On their shared Google calendar, Dina typed in "DTD," which stood for "Do the need," an acronym used with annoying frequency by all the aspiring mothers on the infertility message boards. When they approached one year of trying without success, Garrett said they should talk to a specialist.

"Maybe we should just do IVF," he said.

She was relieved, really, that he'd suggested it. She'd been thinking of it herself but didn't think he'd approve because of the cost—thousands of dollars, along with all their reserves of hope.

"Phil at work, he did that. I mean, his wife did," Garrett said.

"Oh," Dina said, feigning interest in this Phil person.

Just do IVF. Yes, it was expensive. But they had the money. She would gladly sacrifice their annual trips for years to come if she could be a mother. Enough with the ovulation strips and the scheduled sex; they would go the science route. They would make use of technology. Perhaps it was cheating, going against nature, but frankly, Dina didn't care.

The specialist, Dr. Peterson, utilized a PowerPoint presentation with bar charts to explain success rates. On the way home, Dina would say to Garrett, "I'm surprised there was room for us in his office with how big his ego was."

"So, you think there's hope for us?" Dina asked Dr. Peterson.

Hope.

"According to your age, yes. But I need to look at your eggs," he replied.

The dreaded eggs.

He took them to an exam room, and she climbed atop the paper-lined table and put her feet in the stirrups. Garrett sat in a chair positioned directly in front of the stirrups.

"He has the best seat in the house," Dina joked. She wanted to banter with the doctor, like they were on a first date. She wanted them to be friends, as if he could ensure they had a baby if he liked them well enough.

"Look at him, he has no idea where to look right now," Dina continued.

The nurse laughed, but Dr. Peterson was stoic. He inserted the wand, and Dina stared at the screen in front of her, her uterus and ovaries coming into view.

"We've got one follicle on the left, two on the right," Dr. Peterson said to his nurse, who wrote down this information.

"Follicles are good, right?" Dina said.

He removed the wand and stripped off his plastic gloves.

"Yes, follicles are good. We would like there to be more of them."

"Oh, okay," she said. "Like, how many more?"

"I like to see eight to ten," he said. "At least."

Garrett squeezed Dina's toe, as if he was playing "This little piggy went to market." She retracted her foot.

"Eight to ten," Dina repeated.

"The number can vary each month. We can wait for a good month," he said.

Then he gave her a list of supplements that may help her pathetic eggs and suggested she try acupuncture.

"Acupuncture?" she said. "That works?"

He shrugged. "Can't hurt."

She attempted another joke involving needles and how they could, in fact, *hurt*. He didn't laugh.

She ordered all the supplements online, paid an exorbitant fee for expedited shipping. When they arrived, she lined them up on the counter: ubiquinol, myo-inositol, L-arginine, vitamin C, vitamin D, vitamin E, magnesium, pycnogenol, royal jelly. She'd never heard of most of them. She took a baby aspirin too, and 400 percent of the daily recommendation of folic acid. The desperate women on the message boards said wheatgrass was "magical," so she added a scoop of that to her morning smoothies. It tasted like dirt peed on by a pack of dogs.

The acupuncturist was an older Chinese woman who went by Cindy and spoke very broken English. She assured Dina that she would be pregnant within four months. She stuck needles in her feet and abdomen then left her to l still for a half hour. Before Dina went home, Cindy taped tiny metallic balls to the inside of Dina's ear and told her to press on them throughout the day. Supposedly, the ear was a direct line to the uterus and ovaries. Dina wanted to believe. She really did.

Dr. Peterson checked her eggs every month. One month, she had six follicles—six! It was cause for celebration. She started writing a mental draft of a thank-you card to Cindy: *I was skeptical at first, but you made me a believer. We are forever indebted to you.*

"This could be the month," Dina told Garrett. She was giddy. Garrett beamed. Dina had never seen him *beam* before.

"I'll cross my fingers," the nurse said. "We should have your blood work back in a couple hours. If your estrogen levels and FSH levels are within certain limits, you'll start your medications tonight."

The nurse sent them away with a paper bag filled with the injectable medications they would need to stimulate Dina's eggs for IVF, enough to hold her over until her personal shipment arrived. It was five thousand dollars just for the medications; it didn't make sense to purchase them until they were approved to start treatment.

A few hours later, Dina's phone flashed with the doctor's office number. She put the call on speaker so Garrett could hear.

"We got your blood work," said the nurse, a different nurse than earlier. "I'm sorry to say your FSH is still too high to start treatment."

"Oh," Dina said. The tears started coming immediately, plucking-a-nose-hair type tears.

"Maybe next month," the nurse said, trying to be cheerful.

"Probably not," Dina said.

The nurse said "Aww" in a way that made Dina feel worse about herself than she already did. Then she proceeded to rub additional salt in the gaping wound: "We're going to need you to return the loaner medications."

"Right," Dina said. "So you gave me false hope and an errand? Fuck you."

She threw the phone at the floor so hard that the protective case popped off. Garrett jumped to his feet and went to retrieve the phone. It was all he could do to feel like he was helping.

Dina started perusing message boards for women who were not candidates for IVF. Some talked about adoption. Many talked about DEs—donor eggs. She sent messages back and forth with a woman named Gemma whose story sounded so similar to her own—shitty eggs, early menopause, lost cause. Gemma said she wanted to use an egg donor, but her husband was opposed. *He thinks it's too weird*, she wrote. *He's a college professor. I should tell him to just screw one of his students, if he isn't already. He can get her pregnant, and we'll take the kid.* This is what happened to lost-cause women like Dina and Gemma—they went a little nuts.

"So, we get an egg from another woman and join it with my sperm and then you grow the baby?" Garrett said when she explained it to him.

"I know, it's weird," Dina said. "It's basically like you have sex with another woman and I carry the child."

"Except I don't have sex with another woman . . . right?"

He seemed too intrigued for her liking.

"No. Jesus, Garrett."

He shrugged his big, oafy shrug.

There were entire online databases featuring egg donors—twenty-somethings looking to make a quick buck. Dina had been one of these girls once, listed in a database, if they had databases when she was in college; the internet was so young then. It was a cruel kind of irony—the former egg donor in need of eggs.

Stacy caught Dina scrolling through donors while sitting at the nurses' station. It must have looked like Dina was a closet lesbian on a dating site. Dina guessed the donors repurposed their photos from Match.com or wherever. Most of them were in provocative poses.

She tried to have an open mind. But she couldn't find a single donor she liked. The profiles were extremely detailed, with more information than Dina remembered providing when she donated. There was information about the donors' families—most included at least one alcoholic. There was information about the donors' sexually transmitted diseases— an alarming number of them had herpes. Many of them were servers at restaurants with very little education—high school or a couple years at a community college. The best of the bunch had a ring through her septum and an upper leg tattoo. She was getting a graduate degree in psychology.

"What about adoption?" Garrett said.

But Dina had heard horror stories. Some women on the message boards waited years and spent thousands of dollars only to be disappointed. Sometimes, the agencies turned out to be scammers. Sometimes, the birth mothers changed their minds, even after the adoptive parents traveled across the country to be there for the birth. The last thing Dina wanted was more heartache.

Which is why she started fantasizing about stealing a baby.

There were protocols in place to prevent baby stealing, but those protocols protected against the crazed maniacs coming in from off the street looking for an infant. If they tried to take a baby, alarms would sound the second they crossed the painted red lines on the floor in the hallways. Everyone would be alerted to a Code Pink (infant abduction). The poor soul wouldn't make it to the elevator. That system was entirely reliant on identification bands being on the baby. As a nurse, Dina would be the one to attach the requisite identification bands to the baby's wrist and ankle then whisk the baby away to the nursery so the mother could rest. At that point, Dina could cut off the bands, easily. Then they could slip out—her and her baby.

Of course, she couldn't just go home. The hospital would pull security footage, they would see what she'd done. She'd have to go on the run. She'd have to leave Garrett, start a new life with a new name—the whole nine yards. She would lose everything. Except the baby.

*

"So, now what?" Alyssa Delgado says.

It never ceases to amaze Dina how women go from a state of total agony to relaxed bliss after the epidural. She envies the anesthesiologist. He gets more adoration for a few minutes of work than she gets for an entire shift.

"Now we wait," she tells the girl.

"Is that the baby's heartbeat?" the girl asks, tilting her chin toward the screen in front of Dina.

"Yep. It looks good."

"That's good." The girl's phone flashes with a text message. "I guess the parents are on their way."

"Your parents?" Dina says.

The girl laughs. "My parents? That's funny. They pretty much disowned me when *this* happened." She draws an imaginary circle around her belly when she says "this." Then she clarifies: "The adoptive parents."

Dina's heart starts beating fast. She turns her attention to the monitoring screen so the girl can't see the involuntary smile on her face. Adoptive parents. The baby is being given up for adoption anyway. It's as if the universe is giving Dina an encouraging shove—*go, do it, it's meant to be.*

"It's an open adoption," the girl says. "Like in *Juno*."

Dina thinks she's talking about the Alaskan city. She wonders if all adoptions are open there. "Juneau?" she says.

"You know, the movie with the pregnant high-school girl."

"Right," Dina says, though she hasn't seen the movie.

"At least I'm in college. Slightly less scandalous, right?"

Dina glances at the girl's date of birth on her monitoring screen. She's nineteen.

"They put an ad on Craigslist. Isn't that wild?"

Dina has heard of this before, but she still thinks it's ridiculous—people searching for a baby on a website used to sell old refrigerators and arrange casual sexual encounters.

"I guess everything really is online these days," Dina says.

The girl gives a little laugh. "They'd tried agencies before and got screwed or something."

Dina wonders if the adoptive mother is one of the women from the message boards, lamenting all the money and time and hope lost in pursuit of a child through the supposedly proper adoption channels.

"They seem nice. The woman's had a bunch of miscarriages. I felt bad for them," the girl says.

Just look at all the acorns on the forest floor. That's the line Dina gives all the patients who lose babies. She feels for them, but she also envies them in a sick way. At least they've experienced the joy—however temporary—of harboring another life. At least they can get pregnant.

"It's a girl. They're going to name her Caitlin. Caitlin

Rose," Alyssa goes on.

"That's pretty," Dina says, though her real thought is that it's not unique or special enough for a baby so desperately wanted. "I've become such a bitter bitch," Dina had told Garrett the other night. He didn't disagree.

Just as Dina is thinking she wants to ask about the baby's father—who he is, why he isn't here—Alyssa says, "He doesn't even know I got pregnant. The baby's father. In case you're wondering. It's better this way though."

"I'm not here to judge," Dina says, though that's all she does lately—judge.

Alyssa's phone flashes again with another text message.

"They're here," she says.

While the soon-to-be parents make their way to the room, Dina plots how she will steal the baby. Her shift ends in a few hours. It would be ideal if the baby arrived while she was on duty. That does not seem likely, considering how slowly things are progressing currently. If she's not on duty, she will tell Joyce, the nurse scheduled to relieve her, to text her when the baby arrives. Joyce won't be suspicious of this request. Dina is known to be the kind of nurse who cares about her patients. She likes to know that their births go well. She will sneak back into the hospital then wander to the nursery. Someone might say, "I thought you were done for the day," but they wouldn't ask too many questions. At that point, it would be as simple as waiting for an opportunity to cut off the baby's identification bands and then carrying her out, wrapped in the St. Mary's College sweatshirt Dina keeps in her locker.

She regrets that her last words to Garrett were snippy. She didn't know it would be the last time she'd see him. They've been bickering so much lately. They prefer that term—*bickering*—to the more hostile-sounding *fighting*. Maybe he's better off without her. Maybe he'll be relieved when she disappears without a trace.

There's a soft knock on the door.

"Can you let them in?" Alyssa asks.

Dina goes to the door, holding her breath. She is prepared to hate these people. She has to hate them if she is going to rationalize stealing their baby.

The woman is tall, statuesque even. She's too hippy to be a model, but she has a pretty face. The man is short and balding. They do not look like an appropriate match. This helps strengthen Dina's resolve.

"Hello," Dina says with the fakest smile she can muster.

"Hi," the woman says, a huge, genuine smile spreading across her face. "Is this Alyssa Delgado's room?"

"Yes, come in," Alyssa calls out.

The man says, "Pardon us," and they shuffle past Dina. They each assume a post alongside Alyssa's bed.

"How are you feeling?" the woman asks her.

"Fine, now that I have the drugs," Alyssa says.

The three of them laugh.

"I'm sorry, we're so rude," the woman says to Dina. "I'm

Sasha."

"And I'm Jerry," the man says.

They both extend hands to Dina, and she shakes them. They're so polite. Most visitors just ignore the nurse when they descend upon their loved ones. Or they shoo the nurse away—*can you excuse us?*

"That's Dina. I already told her about you guys," Alyssa says.

Dina forces another smile.

"Thank you for taking such good care of our girl," Jerry says to Dina.

Our girl. Dina isn't sure if they're talking about Alyssa or Caitlin Rose.

"Of course," Dina says, fiddling with Alyssa's IV just to have something to do.

"We are just so excited," Sasha says.

Dina doesn't want to hear about their excitement. It will only make her feel guilty about her intentions. So she tells them she has to check on her other patients. "If you need anything, my number is on the whiteboard."

Just as Dina predicted, her shift ends before the baby arrives. Alyssa is dilated six centimeters when Joyce comes on duty. She briefs Joyce on the status of things—baby is tolerating labor well, Alyssa is progressing and her vitals are fine—and then instructs Joyce to text her when the baby comes.

"Thank you so much for everything," Sasha says when Dina is on her way out. Dina plans to go across the street to Denny's to drink coffee and await Joyce's text.

"Just doing my job," Dina says.

There are only a few people at Denny's. They are all sitting alone, drinking coffee. One man has a piece of untouched pie in front of him. Dina decides to use the time to write an email to Garrett. She'll send it once she has baby Caitlin—who shall be renamed—and is on the road. Her plan is to head to Mexico. It's a cliché destination for a fugitive, but it's only a few hours away, and she speaks some Spanish, thanks to her high-school education.

> Dear G,
>
> I am so sorry to do this to you. You know I haven't been myself. This baby thing has ruined me. Maybe now I will be happy. I know it seems awful, what I've done, but I am confident I will give this child the best life possible. I'm sure you'll tell your next wife I'm crazy. That's fine. Please do marry someone else, someone sane and patient and kind. I won't ask you to forgive me, because that seems like an unfair request. How could you? I just ask that you move on, forget me and my lunacy. I did, and do, love you.
>
> xo
>
> D

Just as she finishes the draft, she gets a text from Joyce. "Things moved fast after u left. Baby here. All good."

Dina finishes her coffee and leaves a twenty-dollar bill on the table—a feeble attempt to prove she's a good person.

Nobody looks twice at her when she slips back into the hospital. She's in her scrubs, after all. She just looks like a nurse doing her job. On her own floor, a couple people say hello but don't ask any questions. She swipes her badge to get into the nursery, hoping the baby is there. Some mothers these days ask to keep the baby with them at all times—*rooming in* they call it. Now women are considered bad mothers if they request a few hours of rest away from their newborn. Sasha seems like the type who would encourage Alyssa to rest and then hover over the baby for hours, analyzing every eyelash and fingernail.

Thankfully, the baby is there. Caitlin Rose. Born at 11:37 p.m. Seven and a half pounds. Her swollen eyes are closed, covered in the standard antibiotic goop. She is swaddled tightly, the cheaply made blue-and-pink-striped cap on her head. Dina goes to her, lifts her out of the bassinet. Her heart starts to beat wildly in her chest.

"Getting your daily dose?" a voice says.

She whirls around to see Melissa, one of the pediatric nurses. Melissa smiles warmly, having no idea what Dina's nefarious intentions are.

"Holding them never gets old, does it?" Melissa says.

Dina can feel her lips quiver as she attempts a smile. "Nope, never gets old."

Melissa tends to another baby, and Dina has no choice but to put down Caitlin Rose. She backs out of the nursery, slightly dizzy. What is she doing? She feels suddenly unhinged, embarrassingly so.

In the hallway, outside the nursery, Sasha is crouched with her back against the wall, her head in her hands.

"Sasha?" Dina says. Dina's phone buzzes in her pocket. She ignores it and goes to Sasha. "Are you okay?"

Sasha looks up. "Gosh, I'm such a mess." Her face is red, her eyes watery. "It's just so overwhelming. You have no idea how long we've waited for this."

Dina feels a sting in her throat, the precursor to tears.

"I keep waiting for Alyssa to change her mind. I don't know what I'll do if she changes her mind. Seeing the baby now, I just don't know what I'll do if we lose her."

Dina crouches next to Sasha. She doesn't know what to say, so she just sits there with her. Her phone buzzes again.

"She has a couple days to change her mind," Sasha says. She takes a tissue out of her pocket, dabs at her eyes. "With all the hormones and everything, it just seems like she could change her mind."

"There's nothing that makes me think she will," Dina says.

Sasha nods effusively. "Right, right, that's what Jerry says. I'm just scared."

"Fear comes with motherhood. It's part of the deal," Dina says.

Dina's phone buzzes a third time.

Sasha moves to stand. "I'm sorry you're seeing me like this. You must think I'm such a weirdo."

"No," Dina says. "I really don't."

It's clear now that she can't go back in the nursery. She can't take Caitlin. She just can't.

"I better get back to Jerry," Sasha says. "I told him I was just going to the vending machine. He's seen me cry so many times over not having a baby. Now I have one and I'm crying. The guy can't win."

Sasha manages a small laugh at this, and Dina thinks of Garrett. *The guy can't win.* She's been such a monster to him lately.

"I thought you were off shift," Sasha says as she starts to walk away.

"I am," Dina says. "I thought I forgot something here, but I didn't."

Sasha smiles. "Well, have a good night . . . or day, or whatever it is now. Thank you, again."

Dina watches her walk down the hallway then pulls her phone from her pocket. There are three texts from Garrett, saying he loves her, asking when she's coming home. It's as if he's been a fly on the wall today, observing her insanity. What would he think if she told him she'd considered stealing a baby, fleeing the country, leaving him? She won't tell him.

She will keep this secret. What she will tell him is that she saw her first Craigslist baby. What she will tell him is that anything might be possible.

She texts back:

"I'll be home soon."

proof of errands

HE LIFTED A bag of potting soil into his cart, and Alyssa wondered if his triceps had always been that defined, if they looked that way when he lifted her naked body, all goose-pimply and eager, onto the bed. She used to steal glances in the mirrored closet doors as he rocked into her, but he seemed softer then. Out in the public daylight, his body was different, harder, less susceptible.

"That'll work, right? It says it's for fruits and vegetables. We want to plant herbs," he said.

He was a member of a "we," a "we" she thought was for her. But his "we" always had roots too deep for her to unearth.

Alyssa was just a freshman at UCLA when they met. He was the English teacher all the girls giggled over. It was his shaggy hair and glasses and British accent that made them line up for office hours, asking him for help with their papers. "He's so Hugh Grant-y," Alyssa's classmate had said.

Alyssa stopped by his office twice a week. "Alyssa Delgado," he said every time she darkened his door.

She flirted shamelessly, even though she saw the picture on his desk of him with a woman. "Who's that?" she'd asked, leaning toward the picture in a way she was sure showed off her cleavage.

"Oh, that's Gemma. She's my lady." That's how he'd phrased it—my lady. After several visits to his office, she would learn that he'd met Gemma in grad school and they'd been married seventeen years. "No kids," he'd said, without explanation. After several visits to his office, Alyssa stopped calling him Mr. Eldridge and started calling him Andrew.

On a Friday during office hours, Andrew invited her to his apartment, just a few blocks from campus, to show her his first edition of *Doctor Zhivago*. She went—of course she went. "It's worth four grand," he'd said, impressed with himself. Alyssa had feigned interest in the book, though her only real interest was in Andrew. Gemma wasn't home, was on a writer's retreat all the way across the country, in the Catskills. Alyssa knew the invitation to his house while Gemma was gone had to be by design. She was not surprised when, after sharing a bottle of merlot, he kissed her. She was slightly surprised when they slept together. She was most surprised when it became a regular thing, even after Gemma had returned to California. "Can I come to your place?" he'd ask. And Alyssa would tell her roommate to make herself scarce.

"I want some basil," he said.

Alyssa imagined him stirring it into pasta sauce while Gemma looked on. They would have wine with their dinner. He prided himself on perfect pairings. He'd given Alyssa a bottle of chardonnay once, with a card that said she made him feel brand new. But he won't drink it with her now. He may walk her to her door, but he won't come inside anymore. He doesn't want to see her hairbrush, her bras drying on the towel rack, her unopened mail, her book bag. "We have to put an end to it," he'd said.

"Insects will eat the basil," she told him. But this was of no consequence. He was determined, his ideals already in place.

She followed on his heels, like a lost and lonely puppy— he, her owner, her guardian, the one who would feed her and give her attention before shutting her alone in a dark room for the night. He walked past the lilies, the marigolds, the roses. He used to bring her plants, in an attempt to make her black thumb green, to domesticate her. She didn't mind. She wanted to be domesticated by him. She wasn't ashamed to admit it, though she knew she was supposed to be. She wanted to rub his feet at the end of long days. She wanted to tie his ties. She wanted to make pancakes for him, pancakes with quarter-sized banana slices and walnuts. It wasn't crazy of her to imagine these things. After all, they'd looked in pet stores together, talked about what kind of dog they'd get in some undefined future. He'd wanted a schnauzer, and she'd joked, "You know what they say about men with little dogs." They'd daydreamed of taking his van to all the national parks, starting with Zion. He'd said if they had a daughter together and she inherited Alyssa's big brown eyes, they'd have to worry about the boys calling every day.

He read the tags on the plants, checked the prices, added thyme, rosemary, French tarragon to his cart.

"We have this ledge outside the kitchen window, with a flower box. I told her we could grow herbs in there," he said.

He said these things because they were supposed to have an understanding: he was with Gemma. He strove to breathe life into this fact, constantly resuscitating it, so that the devil on his shoulder could tell the angel, "What? Don't look at me like that. She knows I'm with Gemma. I've been honest." The angel would say, "But Gemma thinks you're just out running errands." The devil would say, "I am, aren't I?"

"It'll be great. I can just reach outside while I'm cooking. A little rosemary here, thyme there," he said.

Alyssa nodded along, refusing to call into question the greatness of it all. Because that's what she did with him. She confirmed. She didn't ask why he thought it made sense to stay married to Gemma instead of falling in love with her. She didn't ask why he'd never made pasta sauce for her.

"Come on," he said, looking toward the warehouse. "I need to find a screen door."

He touched her arm, probably telling himself that he was simply guiding her through the store. The master of justification—they competed for that title. She chastised herself for feeling the adolescent flutter, the hope that what would happen next would mean something, despite all the times it didn't. He would lead her to the back of the store, where the lights were dim and the overstocked paint cans sat, their lids collecting dust. He would express gratitude that she was wearing a skirt, and they would both act like this was just a coincidence, because any suggestion of premeditation made him uneasy. This was, after all, "just one of those things." One of those things that happened in the aisles of home improvement centers, bookstores, markets. Accidentally. Spontaneously. Meaninglessly. The "we" that they were was just two humans keeping each other company, making weekend errands less mundane.

He pressed her up against a wall of tile floor samples. It was after five o'clock. The newlyweds giddy with desire to redo the kitchen floor in their just-purchased condos, the retired couples bored enough to reconsider what they step onto after a long shower—they'd all come earlier in the day, perhaps after reading the Sunday paper together over breakfast at a quaint local diner.

They'd done that once—shared breakfast at a place called the Filling Station. Alyssa paid. He ate half of her French toast, she ate half of his Belgian waffle. It was during his three-week phase of experimental liberation from Gemma, when he was sleeping on an air mattress in a month-to-month studio apartment, like a displaced college student instead of a forty-two-year-old English professor. "It's over with Gemma," he'd told Alyssa. "It's been over." He swore.

During that phase, they looked so good together, his arm around her, when she stole glances in car windows and reflective storefronts, always searching for confirmation of their togetherness. She was always confirming, even when he was denying. Even when he was refusing to sign a long-term lease on an apartment, never explaining what he meant by "I'll wait and see." Even when he was collecting his belongings after a night spent in her bed, not leaving as much as a toothbrush or stray sock, as if he knew that maybe, that day, he'd decide he was done experimenting with liberation, done experimenting with her. Even when he sat on the couch while she cleared the dishes after making roast chicken and corn bread, because sharing soapy water and "I'll wash while you dry" responsibilities would be too intimate. Even when he was rolling her onto her back, never allowing her to be on top, in any sense of the term. Even when he was telling her, when she asked him to meet her parents, "Not today. I have to run a bunch of errands."

Always errands.

His fingers found their way inside her. She wanted to tell him, as she always did in this moment, that she could make him happy, that he should leave Gemma once and for all. But she didn't. Because she knew once she said that, once she compared herself to Gemma, allowed Gemma into this context, he would never call her again. This—his body against hers—was dependent on mutual denial. He pulled her close to him, one leg on either side of his torso. He grabbed her. There was urgency in his eyes. His fingers were trembling against her back now, pressing into her flesh with as much force as when he used to massage her, kneading her muscles until she fell asleep, only to be awakened by him biting her ear.

Alyssa closed her eyes, told herself to enjoy this, this moment. She knew he would go home to Gemma, with his potting soil, his herbs, a screen door. And she would cry in bed alone until sleep rescued her. But the next weekend, when he'd ask if she wanted to come along while he got his car washed or to buy a new barbecue, she would say yes because that feeling of victory as their tongues danced overcame the despair of defeat she felt when he told her he was going back to Gemma. "We have a history," he always said. Seventeen years of sharing electricity bills and secrets and pets and dreams. He'd told Alyssa once, "It's like I'm in a different world with you," and she took it as a compliment. What he meant was that she was a naïve eighteen-year-old, her body taut and breasts firm, a respite from his wife—a brief respite. He could taste the freedom of youth in her mouth. He could pretend to be two decades younger with her, until he couldn't anymore. "Just one of those things," he'd said. Then, unable to let her go completely, he'd added, "But looking at you right now, I wonder if I've made the right decision."

That doubt, his downfall. Alyssa told herself that she agreed to these dalliances, these errands, to hasten the downfall. To hurt him. To worsen his inner conflict, his guilt, his regret. In the dimly lit warehouse, he confessed that seeing her naked body in various poses gave him some of the best visual experiences of his life, and she preyed on this confession, reached into his front pocket, teased him, as if she was just searching for loose change. He sucked on her neck. "God, I want to consume you whole," he whispered, and she found pleasure in his agony. He wanted her, so desperately, and that weakness both repelled and attracted: a scientific impossibility realized. She had yet to learn that his weakness did not make her strong.

He removed one hand from her back, used it to unbutton his jeans. It was fast and dangerous, as it always was. They didn't use a condom. A condom suggested premeditation. When he was done, their bodies separated, and Alyssa's skirt fell back in place. She looked at him, but he wouldn't meet her eyes.

"Excuse me, can I help you with something?" a voice said. It was a kid, not more than sixteen, wearing an orange employee vest.

Andrew pushed Alyssa away so hard she stumbled into a shelf display of paintbrushes. A nailhead rammed into the small of her back.

"I need a screen door," Andrew said to the kid, wiping the sweat from his brow, composing himself. "Five feet by seven feet. Actually, not quite seven feet. Eighty inches. Exactly."

"Sure," the kid said. "You're a few aisles away."

He followed the kid, and she followed him. "I need it for summer. To let in the breeze," he said.

"Well, we have lots of screen door options. We can help you guys out," the kid said.

You guys. Alyssa wanted to tell this guileless kid that they were not a pair, they did not share a home, this was not *their* screen door. She wanted someone, anyone, to judge Andrew.

Alyssa waited while he browsed. She faked interest in light fixtures. Finally, he told her that he was not going to buy a screen door today. He needed to talk about it with Gemma first. It was a more difficult decision than he thought. She followed him to the car. He opened the trunk and lifted the potting soil inside then carefully wedged the herbs, in their plastic containers, between the side panels and the soil. Such care he gave to the future occupants of his planter.

"Thanks for coming with me," he said once his key was in the ignition. Alyssa sat in the passenger's seat, where Gemma would sit. A strand of long black hair hung from the door handle. One of Gemma's, no doubt. The light caught it just so, revealing a slight reddish tint. Alyssa hoped it was dyed, fake, an illusion. There was a can of Diet Coke in the cup holder, lipstick on the edge, and a receipt from the car dealership in the center console. Both of their names were on it: Gemma and/or Andrew Eldridge. There were two tennis rackets in the back seat.

He ran a red light on his way to drop off Alyssa at her apartment. It was ten 'til six. He'd probably told Gemma he'd be home by six. To make dinner. He didn't want to be late. Alyssa hoped for more lights to turn red, but there was a series of green, and she hated him for his luck, his ability to sidestep consequences. He would return to Gemma, with his purchases, his props to rationalize his absence. He had receipts, conscience-easing bags of evidence. He'd killed the proverbial two birds with one stone.

He pulled in front of Alyssa's building, didn't even put the car in park while she got out. She smoothed her hair, hoping, as she always did, to entice him to come inside. But his foot was firmly on the brake, ready and waiting to be on the gas again.

"Have a good night," she said politely, calmly. She didn't want him to know that she'd go inside and cry.

"You too," he said.

She uncorked the bottle of chardonnay he'd given her. She didn't know why she'd saved it all this time. Or she did know why, but she was too ashamed of the reasons, of how she'd imagined they would share it, get so sloppy drunk that they'd stumble to the bedroom, fall to the floor, and get naked next to the closet. He'd yank her wool-lined winter jacket from its hanger, insist she lie on it. Because in her fantasies, her comfort was his utmost concern.

Near the end of the bottle, there was a knock at the door. When he called for her—"Alyssa, are you there?"—she scolded her drunken mind for playing this cruel trick. He knocked again, and she found herself turning the knob to let him in.

He was standing there in the same jeans and faded Pink Floyd T-shirt he had been wearing earlier. A dish towel, spotted with blood, was wrapped around his hand.

"What happened?" she asked. Her words sounded as if they were coming from a megaphone three feet behind her. She would be hungover tomorrow. She instinctively took his wound into her hand.

"I was slicing open the bag of soil with a steak knife and, I don't know, Gemma was asking me where I'd been, and I got nervous or something. Nearly took the top off my index finger." He gave her the same smile he gave her when he led her to the back of those warehouses. "I told her I'd take myself to the hospital. My fault, you know. I'm the clumsy idiot."

"So, what are you doing here?"

"Come with me. We'll get a drink or something. Go out for once. I told her it could be hours at the hospital."

"Well, it could."

"It's not that bad, the cut. I made it seem worse than it is," he said. He was right. It wasn't that bad. "Let's just go to the drug store. We'll pick up some gauze, some bandages. You can make it look professional. Then we can go to that bar downtown."

Our bar, Alyssa thought. He would get the table in the back, order two vodka sodas. Under the table, his hand would find her thigh, his fingers would walk inside her, and their stoic faces would never let on. He would tell her to meet him in the bathroom, because he knew their bar had a single bathroom that locked to the outside world. There was always a line. He would hoist her up on the sink, pull her into him. Her backbone would scrape against the faucet. He would leave. She would leave two minutes later. Because he cared what strangers thought. They would finish their drinks, and he would drive her home, thank her for coming with him. She would send him on his way, after applying his bandages of course.

"I can't," she said. Denying him sobered her up faster than a cold shower.

"You can't?" He looked confused.

"Not tonight," she said, because she wasn't ready to tell him, or herself, that she didn't want to see him again. For now, all she wanted was to send him home, drunk with a dose of his own medicine, and let him bleed. For once.

"So, I really have to go to the hospital?" he said with a sly smile.

"You said it yourself—it's not that bad," she said. "Just one of those things."

the duck in the kitchen

THERE IS A duck in Garrett's kitchen. A live one. And it didn't waddle in from the backyard of his suburban tract home. He put it there. Right there on the counter. It's shuffling back and forth, from the toaster to the blender, its amphibian-looking webbed feet making the same sound on the Formica countertop as Dina's feet make on the tile floor when she gets out of the shower in the morning. What is he going to tell Dina? *Honey, I brought home a duck! I know it's no replacement for the baby we can't have, but isn't it cute?*

It's not like he woke up this morning and decided he would return home with a duck. That would be strange. This was a sensible decision, rational even, given the circumstances.

This morning, his alarm beeped three times at 6:15 a.m. and he hit snooze, which Dina hates. *Why don't you just set the alarm for six thirty if you're going to just hit snooze anyway?* He's explained to her that he likes the feeling of snoozing, of defying the authority of the alarm, of sneaking in that fifteen minutes of sleep. It's one of the only true luxuries of his day. There was a time, not that long ago, when Dina found these quirks of his charming. Now he just irritates her. She's not going to understand the duck.

This morning, he actually hit snooze twice—a rarity. He was especially tired, after a night of lying awake, thinking about what Dina had said at dinner: "If we can't have a baby, what's the point of even being married?" He wasn't sure if she meant it, or if she was just frustrated. This baby thing has overtaken their lives. He doesn't even care if they are childless at this point; he just wants his wife back. Or, rather, the not-crazy version of his wife. He can't call her that to her face—crazy. He made that mistake once, saying something like, "Honey, you're acting crazy." She didn't talk to him for two days, just stomped around the house, communicating via slamming cabinets and doors and drawers. She has gone crazy, though. It's just a fact. Maybe he's gone crazy too. Hence, the duck.

Last night's insomnia was especially stubborn. He tried counting sheep, even entertained himself with penguins and elephants and field mice. He searched the cottage cheese ceiling for shapes, finding an oak tree, a seahorse, and a Grateful Dead bear. He played games with the clock, guessing the hour, telling Insomnia that if he was within ten minutes of the right time, he "won" and should be allowed to sleep. Insomnia does not play by any rules though.

Dina didn't sleep either. It would make sense for them to keep each other company during these stressful, sleepless hours, but she just turned on her side away from him, sighing occasionally to let him know that she was, in fact, awake, just choosing not to engage with him. This is what their marriage has become.

They ate breakfast together in the morning, pretending to be a normal, loving couple. Before the Baby Project, they used to chat about their upcoming days, discuss what take-out they would order for dinner. Now they stare at their respective bowls of cereal, in silence except for the clinking of their spoons.

They should probably see a marriage counselor. The fertility doctor had recommended that: "This is very hard on many couples." Dina says it will be a waste of time and money though: "We can't have a baby. That's the problem. Not sure how a therapist is going to fix that."

They gave each other perfunctory kisses goodbye before heading out to their respective jobs. Dina works in Labor and Delivery at Cedars-Sinai, which must be torture for her. Garrett has tried to suggest she take a position on a different unit, but she says she's not going to let the Baby Project dictate her life. As if it's not doing that already.

Garrett has started seeing his commute as forty minutes of freedom. It used to be forty minutes of drudgery. This shift in perspective reminds him of how unpleasant his life has become. The commute is only eight miles, meaning he travels at a rate of five minutes per mile. He's convinced he could run faster than that, or he could if he didn't spend nine hours a day immobile behind a desk, his muscles atrophying.

Frazier Investment Group occupies three floors of a high-rise, including the coveted twelfth-floor penthouse. Every day, Garrett pulls into the parking garage at precisely 7:51 a.m., this day being no exception. He swiped his entrance card after waiting in the usual line while others swiped their cards. He can never understand why people take so long, digging through purses and fumbling under car seats. His card is always in the cup holder, easily accessible. He never holds up the line.

There is always a little "thought of the day" by the swiper. Today's was "In the US, one pound of potato chips costs 200 times more than two pounds of potatoes." There was no citation. He found this hard to believe. Yesterday's "thought" was "Only female mosquitoes bite." He told Dina about that one, and she snapped, "I'm sure you think that's funny." He really wasn't trying to imply anything.

It takes exactly three minutes to get to the third level of the parking structure. He doesn't know who comes in before eight, but apparently enough people to fill two levels. He wonders if these people work at Frazier, if their early arrivals are earning them promotions he is routinely denied. He parked in the same spot as always, next to the same Volvo station wagon with one of those shades on the window, used to protect babies from abusive sunbeams.

Some take the stairs, some take the elevator, but every morning they all converge on the one path into the building, carrying briefcases and coffee mugs, some of them already talking on phones or scrolling through emails. Nobody speaks, not even when they load into the elevator to go to their respective floors. Recently, the building manager installed TV screens in the elevators, flashing last night's sports scores and a few news headlines. Everyone pretends to be enthralled so they don't have to communicate.

Garrett works on the tenth floor, so he closes his eyes and waits while the elevator stops every ten seconds, disposing of occupants. This morning, he nearly fell asleep standing up. It was the guy next to him clearing his throat that startled him back to alertness. He made a mental note to sanitize his hands, in case the throat-clearing signified a respiratory illness.

He logged on to his computer—password Dina&G, remnants of a happier time—before he even put down his briefcase, because he wanted "the system" to know he arrived at 7:57 a.m., before Kenji and the other ass-kissers. His cubicle is a "corner cube," though the term "cube" is misleading. A true cube would have a ceiling. Garrett would prefer a ceiling, to be completely enclosed and hidden. His corner cube has not one, but two windows. Windows are considered a special privilege. Kenji is deeply resentful of Garrett's two windows.

Garrett never does any work before nine. The first hour of the day is spent paying bills and watching the previous night's episode of *The Late Show* online. When the Baby Project began, the first hour of his day was dedicated to reading articles about infertility that Dina sent him. She doesn't send those anymore—either because there are no more left on the internet (her search was exhaustive) or because she's given up.

The work emails really get going around 9:15 a.m. This morning, Receptionist Tracy alerted everyone to the presence of bagels and various flavors of cream cheese in the conference room. Within five seconds of her email, heads appeared over the tops of un-ceilinged cubicles as if a preacher had just said "All rise" at Sunday mass. It's amazing, the allure of breakfast foods. Garrett was not interested, though, because he didn't want to have to make small talk with anyone while obtaining his bagel.

Phil emailed both Garrett and Jake about their joint effort on a profit-and-loss statement for one of their new funds. The subject line: *Just checking in*. Phil was always *just checking in*. Right as Garrett was having this thought, Jake emailed: "Hey, just checking in on Phil's 'just checking in' email." Garrett laughed out loud, for what felt like the first time in a year. He's always liked Jake. Jake is younger, but he's not one of those hungry go-getters hopped up on Red Bull and ambition. In a strange moment of male sharing, Garrett had told Jake that he and Dina were "trying" but "struggling." Jake gave him a look of genuine sympathy and said, "My wife and I went through some stuff. And now she's due in a few weeks. So hang in there."

Garrett went home to Dina that night and told her this story of hope. She'd said, "Don't talk to me about pregnant women."

Garrett pulled up his requisite Excel spreadsheets and stared at his computer screen for a good five minutes. The staring was only interrupted by his desk phone ringing—Kenji. Kenji's cube is just twenty feet away, but he insists on calling.

"What's up, Kenji?"

"You didn't want a bagel? There are all kinds—cranberry, sesame, garlic—"

"Maybe later."

"They might be gone."

"Kenji, is this why you called?"

"Well, no, actually I was wondering if your desk was cleaned last night."

All employees have these placards that say please clean my desk that they're supposed to leave out when they want the night crew to Lysol their keyboards and Windex their computer screens. Garrett does not leave out his placard because he has a feeling they spit on the keyboards and computer screens, because that's what he would do in response to a placard's command. Dina says he has "passive-aggressive energy," and maybe she's right.

"I don't know, Kenji. I never put up my sign."

"*Never*? I saw this segment on *Good Morning America*

about bacteria in the workplace. Your keyboard is probably more infested than the toilet seat."

"And yet I am still alive."

"Alright, I'll ask Jake about his desk. It looks like they didn't clean."

Kenji hung up, and Garrett resumed staring at his screen. He hasn't been able to find the will to work lately. Maybe it's fatigue. He *is* tired—of Dina, of life, of mundanity. He started counting every time the cursor blinked and got all the way to two hundred before his eyes started to burn, and he wondered if anyone would notice if he ducked under his desk to take a nap. What would he say if someone caught him? *Oh, I was just practicing in the event of an earthquake.*

The ding of a meeting request snapped him out of his stupor. It was from Andrea, also known as the Fridge Nazi. It said "Urgent kitchen maintenance meeting" and was scheduled for 11:00 a.m. There was a red exclamation mark next to the invite, which Garrett thinks people use too liberally these days, creating a "boy who cries wolf" scenario. What could be so urgent about kitchen maintenance? He looked at his options: Accept, Tentative, Decline. Then he hit Decline. He felt a rush similar to the rush of snoozing. That rush motivated more defiance. He set his "out of office" alert to say he was at an important client meeting. And he left.

He thought he'd do a few laps around the man-made lake in the business park, get some exercise for endorphins. When he started at Frazier, they gave him a brochure for the business park that featured the lake and its surrounding walking path and benches. It said "An idyllic getaway from the workday." Garrett goes there at lunch sometimes and, more often than not, circles the lake while pretending to talk on his phone. This serves two functions: One, nobody bothers him if they think he is engaged in conversation. And two, in his fake conversation, he can vent to the supposed person on the other line. He has talked to this imaginary person at length about the Baby Project. It's like therapy without the couch and expense.

At 10:55 a.m., he was the only person at the lake, so he didn't have to engage in fake conversation. The ducks, sleeping peacefully on the water, opened their eyes, no doubt confused by a human's presence at this unusual hour. The poor ducks. Garrett never knew ducks could be overweight until he started working at Frazier. They are plump, enlarged by the lunchtime leftovers of the cubicle dwellers who find it amusing to feed them chow mein noodles and burrito drippings. Garrett once eavesdropped on a conversation between two mailroom guys who, upon disposing of a Chicken McNugget in the lake, pondered whether or not a duck consuming McDonald's poultry would qualify as cannibalism. They smelled like weed—the guys, not the ducks.

He pities them, the ducks. He often imagines them flying overhead, spotting the glossy, shimmering lake below, protected by the surrounding tall buildings, sheltered from the winds. From up there, the corporate world must look promising, real, fulfilling—so they flock. And so they arrive, with families in tow. The lake is cleaned weekly. Plants are placed in the water—lily pads too—to simulate the lakes they'd come from, the dirtier, riskier lakes. The groundskeepers put out grain every day. There are no dogs running about, like in recreational settings, none of the usual predators. And there are plenty of well-manicured bushes where they can lay their eggs. So they decide to stay—not because they like it, but because they know it's safe, secure.

This day, on his walk around the lake during the kitchen maintenance meeting, he spotted three broken eggs on the ground. He was perplexed, confused as to the origins of these eggs until he saw the remnants of a nest a few feet away. He knew then that something horrible had happened.

Behind him, a quack. He turned to see a female duck. He knew it was a female because of its brown-speckled plumage. For some reason, Mother Nature made the female ducks less striking than the emerald-necked males. Maybe it was so they could be easily camouflaged while nesting, for safety. This duck's nest was not safe though. Garrett's best guess was that a curious squirrel had come along and dashed this duck's hope for a family.

He crouched next to the duck. She didn't move. He reached out to her, surprised she let him stroke her feathers. She seemed to enjoy it even. He knows Dina will think this sounds insane, but it's like they understood each other. He's not exactly sure what came over him, but he put one hand underneath the duck's bosom and lifted her. He was surprised at how heavy she was. She quacked once, more in surprise than protest. It was like she wanted him to take her. Dina will think that's insane too.

He told himself if the duck struggled at all in his grasp, he would let it go and return to the tenth floor. But she didn't struggle and, just like the phenomenon of not remembering the roads taken but somehow arriving home, he found himself in the driver's seat of his car, with the duck as his passenger.

And now he finds himself in his kitchen. With a duck.

It's late, past midnight. Dina should have been home from work hours ago. Maybe she really is leaving him. If she does come home, she's not going to be pleased. This duck is not the way to close the chasm that has formed between them. Unless she finds it hilarious and starts laughing uncontrollably. But he can't imagine Dina laughing uncontrollably. It would be something if she did.

He could shoo the duck into the backyard and hope she finds a neighbor's pool to call home. He could pretend this whole thing never happened and not mention it to Dina. But he's starting to think he should return the duck to the corporate lake. It's possible the duck is missing her mate. According to Google, ducks are monogamous, at least for the duration of a season. If the duck in his kitchen reunites with her lover-of-the-season, they can make more babies. They can have their family.

He texts Dina:

"All OK? You coming home?"

There is no response. Maybe she decided to work a double shift. Still, he knows she carries around her phone at work, in the pocket of her scrubs. When they were dating, she responded to texts right away. They volleyed playful messages back and forth. He smiled through his days at Frazier then.

He sends another text:

"I know you've been upset lately. I'm sorry I don't always say the right thing. I love you, sweetie."

The duck continues walking back and forth on the counter, emitting a quack occasionally. She does not seem distressed. Bored, if anything. Garrett sets out a bowl of water then googles what to feed the duck. Google recommends oats, peas, and corn. He defrosts a small bowl of frozen peas and corn then tops the veggies with a handful of oats.

His muscles tense as he waits for Dina to respond. He feels like he's just one text away from her saying something devastating like "I can't do this anymore." He doesn't want to think about returning to his bachelor life, a life with Hot Pockets and too many beers and, quite possibly, this duck. If she wants a child, they should adopt. Yes, it's a crapshoot. Yes, it could lead to more disappointment and heartache, but they should at least try. It would be the Baby Project 2.0: The

New Frontier. This project could bond them. Of course, if it doesn't work out, as the Baby Project 1.0 has not worked out, it could destroy them. But they are close to destroyed anyway.

He sends a third text:

"I want to pursue adoption. I've decided. Can we talk about it when you get home?"

Dina always says he's too passive. This is his attempt at being not-passive, a Hail Mary in their marital dynamic.

Finally, she responds:

"I'll be home soon."

This tentative acceptance of his invitation to talk is the closest they've come to affection in weeks. He lifts the duck off the counter, tells her, "Can you stay in the garage for a bit?" He will take her back to the lake in the morning. If the adoption conversation goes well, if it ends with him and Dina holding hands on the couch, committed to the Baby Project 2.0, he will tell Dina about the duck. "So, I have a funny story," he'll say. She will raise her eyebrows in anticipation, and he will tell her. And she will laugh, buoyed by the hope of their new project. She will laugh so hard that she collapses into him, happy tears at the corners of her eyes.

the exchange

JILLIAN SITS IN the parking lot, eyes on the entrance to Starbucks. She's early, as planned. She knew she'd need some time to compose herself. She looks around the parking lot, wondering if Sasha is also early, sitting in her own car, taking deep breaths. It's weird, this meetup. She wonders how many like it have happened in other coffee shops. She watches a woman go into the Starbucks. She's alone. It could be Sasha. She's petite, with blonde hair cut in a cute bob. Jillian has no idea what Sasha looks like. This woman is the right age—late thirties, early forties—but she looks too composed to be a new mother. Not five minutes later, the woman exits the shop, latte or whatever in one hand, cell phone in another, pressed to her ear. Not Sasha.

Jillian texts Matt:

"Going in now"

Matt wasn't sure she should do this, thought it would make her too emotional. But Jillian's confident she's already explored the depths of her sorrow, hit bottom. She knows there's no place deeper to go. It's liberating, in a way.

Matt texts her a fist bump emoji.

The Starbucks is empty, except for the two employees working at the counter laughing about something on one of their phones. One of them—a rail-thin college-aged kid with bleached blond hair and a hole in his chin, probably for a piece of jewelry disallowed by the employee handbook—looks up and says, "Oh hey, can I help you?" The other, an Asian girl with a long black braid down her back, suspiciously eyes the ice chest resting on Jillian's forearms.

Jillian orders a chamomile tea. Her nerves can't handle coffee. She claims a table and sets the ice chest on a chair then retrieves her tea, removing the lid to allow the steam to escape. She sits, fiddles with her phone, mindlessly scrolling Instagram, even though all the photos of happy families are torture. Matt says she needs to delete the app, but she never does. It's like she's constantly picking at an open wound, preventing it from scabbing over, healing.

She plays a round of Words with Friends against Matt. She always beats him, and he always says her streak is about to end.

The sound of street noise alerts her to the fact that the door has opened. She looks up to see a tall woman enter. The woman glances around the room, nervousness on her face. Her eyes meet Jillian's, and they both smile tentatively.

The woman approaches.

"Are you Jillian?" she asks.

The two Starbucks employees pause their conversation to observe this awkwardness. They must be wondering if this is a first date.

Jillian half stands from the table and says, "Yes. Sasha?"

Sasha nods, hangs her purse over the chair, and then wraps her arms around Jillian.

Jillian isn't prepared for this—physical contact with a stranger. They've chatted online, shared their respective stories, so they aren't total strangers, but still. Some months ago, at the ad agency where Jillian works, they did this team-building exercise, asking everyone to submit responses to a questionnaire to reveal what color personality they had. Jillian was a "blue," meaning she prefers alone time. In the section with tips on how to interact with her, it said "Do not touch her, if you can avoid it."

"It's so wonderful to meet you," Sasha gushes.

Jillian feels her cheeks redden. She's normally a shy person. Everything about this is not who she is.

"You too," she says.

The two women sit. Jillian takes a sip from her tea, so she has something to do. She didn't wait long enough though; she burns the tip of her tongue and winces.

"You didn't bring Caitlin," Jillian says.

Caitlin Rose is Sasha's new baby. After years of trying to have their own, Sasha and her husband decided on adoption. Jillian received a handful of emails in response to her ad. She chose Sasha because she knew a thing or two about struggle, loss, heartache.

"No, I wasn't sure if that was a good idea," Sasha says.

Jillian wonders if Sasha pities her, if she thinks Jillian can't tolerate the sight of a baby. She resents this, even though she knows she would have resented Sasha for bringing the baby too.

"She's fussy, is what I mean," Sasha says, as if reading Jillian's mind.

Jillian releases her resentment, takes solace in the fact that women who have spent any time in this hell of grief understand each other.

"Well, she's just been in the world a few days. I'd be fussy too," Jillian says.

"I've been in this world almost forty years, and I'm still fussy."

They laugh. Like the hug, Jillian hadn't anticipated this. It was just a month ago when she was sure she'd never laugh again.

Jillian's doctor's office was right next to a specialty health food store that sold things like seventeen-dollar bags of organic Marcona almonds and eight-dollar smoothies the color of swamp water. She used to make fun of places like this, roll her eyes at people who lived on massaged kale and kimchi. It was so LA. She'd lived in Los Angeles her whole life but prided herself on being anti-everything LA represented:

celebrity, diets, fake boobs, faker smiles.

But when she got pregnant, she found herself slipping into the health food store before her appointments and getting one of the eight-dollar smoothies. They tasted better than they looked and claimed all kinds of nutritional benefits. She'd look at her starting-to-protrude stomach and say, "This is for you, peanut."

She was in this very health food store at twenty-three weeks pregnant, looking at the selection of vegan protein bars in the ten minutes she had to spare before her doctor's appointment, when she got a sudden feeling of something being off. There was no other way to put it—just *off*. She was glad she happened to have an appointment, just to make sure everything was okay. If she was coming down with a cold, she wanted to ask what she could take for it. She hoped it was nothing. She didn't feel comfortable even popping a Tylenol, had become the holistic weirdo she'd never taken seriously.

She chitchatted with the women at the front desk in the doctor's office. One of them was drinking kombucha—probably from the health food store—and said she felt strange from it.

"Well, there's a little alcohol in it," the heavyset woman said.

"There *is*?" the other woman said. They inspected the label and both started laughing. "Doesn't take much to get me buzzed, I guess."

"Cheap date."

Jillian laughed good-naturedly but started to wonder if her smoothie had kombucha in it, if she'd unknowingly ingested some alcohol. It would explain that *off* feeling. She sat in the waiting room, googling "alcohol in kombucha," feeling slightly relieved when she saw how small the percentage was. She'd ask the doctor about it anyway.

The nurse called her back and showed her to the bathroom—always the first stop during these appointments. There were several plastic cups stacked next to the toilet. Jillian wrote her last name and the date on one then peed into it and left it in the small pass-through window between the bathroom and the nurse's station—like a drive-through window for urine, Jillian always thought.

When she came out, she got on the scale—she'd gained twelve pounds so far. The nurse said, "Very good," then took her blood pressure, which was also "very good." In the exam room, Jillian sat on the paper-lined table, waiting for the doctor. She loved ultrasounds—hearing the heartbeat, seeing her tiny person swimming around.

Dr. Wong was a forty-something Chinese woman. She always wore a white lab coat, black pencil skirt, nylons, and black pumps. Jillian guessed she wore this uniform even in the delivery room. She'd told Matt she hoped she went into labor in the middle of the night so she could see Dr. Wong's casual attire.

"How's it going, Jillian?" Dr. Wong said, taking that extra moment to look Jillian in the eye before glancing at the chart in her hand.

"Good. I feel a little off today, like I might be coming down with something. But everything is good overall."

"Glad to hear. Let's take a look at the baby."

Dr. Wong sat on a stool on wheels and rolled up next to the exam table. Jillian folded down the waistband of her skirt, bared her growing belly. Dr. Wong squirted on the gel then spread it around with the wand.

There was the heartbeat—strong and steady. Jillian smiled.

"Huh," Dr. Wong said, leaning in closer to the screen.

Jillian felt the tiny muscles holding up her smile suddenly atrophy.

"What is it?"

Dr. Wong wore one of those red string bracelets around her wrist, which made Jillian believe she was spiritual, in touch with something bigger than herself. Jillian guessed that's why she was always so calm, unruffled. She'd never seen her worried or bothered until this very moment.

"I'm not sure. I'm going to check your cervix, okay?" Dr. Wong said.

Usually, for this exam, the doctor would instruct Jillian to undress and drape her lower half with a paper skirt of sorts. Then she would step out to give Jillian privacy. Dr. Wong didn't step out though. She just handed Jillian the paper skirt and waited.

Jillian didn't get off the table, just wriggled out of her

skirt and underwear and covered herself with the paper. Dr. Wong told her to lie down, to scoot to the end of the table. Jillian felt Dr. Wong's fingers go inside her, and she held her breath.

"We need to get to the hospital," Dr. Wong said, standing from her stool on wheels and taking off her plastic gloves.

Jillian pushed up onto her elbows. "What is it?"

"You're four centimeters dilated, and your water bag is dropping."

This information made no sense. All Jillian could manage was "What?"

"You're in labor," Dr. Wong said.

She opened the door and called out to the nurse. The nurse rushed in and told Jillian to call Matt. When she did, she told him to come to the office and the nurse said, "Oh, no, honey, there's no time for that. Tell him to go straight to the hospital."

They called an ambulance, put her inside. Dr. Wong held her hand on the way.

"Is she going to be okay?" Jillian asked Dr. Wong.

The baby was a girl. They'd found that out weeks ago, when they did the blood testing to make sure there were no chromosomal defects. Jillian had been eager to post their pregnancy announcement on social media but wanted to wait until they knew the baby was healthy. They were supposed to be able to celebrate after those blood tests came back; they were supposed to be able to stop worrying. Jillian had even changed her username on Instagram to @JillianPlusOne.

Matt had been coaching soccer at the local high school when she'd told him to come to the hospital. When they wheeled her to the Labor and Delivery unit, he was standing there, still in his cleats, his hair wet with sweat.

"What's going on?" he said. His eyes were wild, crazed. She'd never seen him like this before.

"I'm in labor, I guess," she said, trying to keep her tone light. *There has to be a way they can stop this*, she thought. She'd had friends who needed to get some kind of injection to stop preterm contractions; she assumed there were similar medical interventions that would help her.

But it seemed the only intervention they had was adjusting the bed so that her head was lower than her feet, hoping gravity would help keep the baby inside. Gravity—the most rudimentary of tools.

They pumped her full of drugs that made her limbs feel heavy and her heart feel light. She couldn't lift her head to eat or drink.

The nurse, a middle-aged woman named Wendy, sat with her, holding her hand, as day turned to night.

"Is there really nothing they can do?" Jillian asked Nurse Wendy.

She didn't answer with a yes or no. She just said, "I'm so sorry, sweetheart."

Jillian cried. Matt held her other hand, squeezed it tightly.

"Let's just take it one hour at a time," Nurse Wendy said. "Each hour she stays inside is an accomplishment."

Dr. Wong disappeared from the scene. Jillian was too out of it to ask why. The neonatal doctor came in around ten o'clock. He explained that preterm labor at twenty-three weeks was a notorious gray area. "At twenty-two weeks, babies don't have a chance, frankly. At twenty-four weeks, they do, but there are such high risks of disability," he said. Jillian couldn't concentrate. She heard certain words—"blindness," "cerebral palsy," "brain bleed"—but they sounded like they were being said to someone else, at the other end of a long hallway.

At the end of the diatribe, Matt spoke. His voice sounded louder, closer than the doctor's. "We want to do everything we can for this baby," he said. He didn't need to consult Jillian on this declaration; he knew she'd agree.

The goal became to keep the baby inside as long as possible. The first three days in the hospital were encouraging. The baby's heartbeat was strong and steady. Friends and family members were sending emails and texts, saying they were praying. Jillian and Matt didn't sleep—how could they? The nurses kept Jillian on a steady diet of magnesium sulfate in the hopes of slowing the labor. They gave her steroid injections in her butt to help the baby's lung development.

Matt was on his phone constantly, looking up stories of other parents in their situation—success stories. He shared them with Jillian, dared to get her hopes up. One of Jillian's coworkers left a voice message to say, "I just wanted to tell you that I was born at twenty-five weeks. There is hope!" Jillian couldn't help but think ahead to telling their baby the story of her terrifying entrance into the world. She couldn't help but think of their baby growing up to tell others, "I was born at twenty-three weeks!"

On their third day, though, things took a turn. Jillian had been having contractions for days but couldn't feel them until that third day in the hospital. Then there was blood.

"I'm going to call your doctor," Nurse Wendy said.

Matt turned on the TV, a lame attempt at distraction.

When Dr. Wong arrived, she did an ultrasound that revealed the water bag was continuing to move down, bringing their baby with it. The baby's heartbeat was still strong and steady. She was squirming around, kicking wildly, full of life.

"Look at her," Matt said, smiling, seemingly forgetting their reality for just a moment.

Just then Jillian saw the baby's foot kick through her cervix. Dr. Wong sighed.

"This baby is coming," Dr. Wong said.

The baby was breech, and her body was far too fragile to survive delivery. If there was any chance at life, they needed to do a C-section. Because of the baby's size, the doctor wanted to do a classical C-section, which involves a long, vertical incision giving the doctor more access to the uterus. The doctor said this meant Jillian could never have a vaginal birth for any future children; the risk of uterine rupture was too high. They made Jillian sign something, acknowledging, consenting.

Nurse Wendy looked Jillian deep in the eyes. "No matter what happens, treasure today, okay? This is the day you meet your baby."

Jillian nodded, taking these as formal instructions, thinking if she obeyed them, a miracle would happen.

They prepped her for surgery, starting an aggressive IV of magnesium to protect the baby's brain. Jillian drank something that would prevent her from vomiting and choking during the C-section. She tried to move her hands and realized she couldn't. When she looked down, they were clenched into fists.

"I can't move my hands," she told Matt, panicking.

"It's probably anxiety, hon," one of the other nurses, Dina, said, before ordering Jillian to give her jewelry to Matt.

The operating room was cold and sterile. There was so much commotion. Jillian closed her eyes but then opened them because the darkness scared her. Someone told her to breathe, which she thought was absurd. Then it was silent.

Then she heard a splash, her water breaking.

"She's out, she's out," the doctor said.

"She's trying to cry," one of the nurses said.

Nurse Wendy leaned over the curtain and said, "She's so cute, Jillian. She's breathing. She's crying. Can you hear her?"

Jillian could hear her. She mewed like a kitten.

She weighed 1 pound and 4 ounces. She was 10.1 inches long. Her first Apgar score was 8, her second was 9. Jillian felt a surge of pride for this—her little baby, coming into the world so strong.

They named her Evin. It hadn't been on the list of names they were considering. Matt had found it online, in those two days they were waiting in the hospital for whatever was going to happen next. "It means 'young fighter,'" he'd said.

A few hours after Evin was born, after a team of people whisked her away to the NICU, Nurse Wendy came to Jillian's bedside.

"This is for you," she said, handing her a small heart, cut from blue-and-white polka-dot fabric. There was a note pinned to it, instructing Jillian to wear the heart against her skin for a day or two then place it in Evin's Isolette so she could sense her mother's nearness. Jillian would find out later that fellow NICU moms cut out these hearts for others who would reluctantly join their club. They wanted to keep their hands busy during all the hours of waiting and worrying.

Jillian pumped breast milk feverishly. It was all she could do to help Evin, so she did it every hour, on the hour. She visited Evin as often as possible, watching the nurses check her tiny baby's oxygen levels and give her medications and take x-rays and adjust the ventilator. They changed her diapers—her impossibly small diapers—and swabbed breast milk into her mouth. Evin gave the sweetest suck.

It was just ten hours after she was born that the neonatal doctor told Jillian and Matt that Evin's lungs were too premature. There was nothing to be done, he said. Evin would not survive, he said.

They hovered over Evin's Isolette, their tears falling onto the plastic.

"Do you want to hold her?" one of the nurses, Melissa, asked.

Jillian and Matt looked up simultaneously. "Can we?" they asked, in unison.

Nurse Melissa removed Evin from her Isolette, wrapped her in a blanket, and settled her in Jillian's arms. Jillian had to sit—not only because she'd just undergone surgery, but because she was dizzy with too many emotions. There was overwhelming sadness, of course. But also joy. Mother Nature had programmed women to feel this when holding their babies for the first time, even if it was also the last time.

"Her oxygen saturations are higher than they've been," Nurse Melissa said softly.

This fact confirmed that Evin wanted to be with her parents. She was safest there. She was comforted there.

As her heartbeat slowed and faded, the nurses took Evin's

footprints and handprints. Then Matt and Jillian bathed Evin, admiring every inch of her. After the bath, Jillian put a diaper on her, as if she were like any other baby post-bath, then swaddled her tightly. They kissed her forehead and whispered their love for her. They told her not to be afraid, that they would see her again one day. In an instant, they'd become devout believers in heaven. Evin took her last breath resting against Jillian's breast. Before they took her away, Jillian removed the fabric heart from inside her bra and tucked it into Evin's swaddle.

They buried her in the cemetery near their house. Jillian told Matt that they can never move now. As much as they've said they hate Los Angeles, they are now permanent residents. They visit the grave at least once a week. Sometimes Jillian goes by herself and doesn't tell Matt. She doesn't want to worry him. She knows he wants her to move on.

When they got home from the hospital, Jillian kept pumping, toting the compact machine around like it was an oxygen tank keeping her alive. At first, she told Matt it was because her boobs were so engorged; she had to relieve them. But after a week of pumping around the clock, they both knew it was more than that. She pumped milk because it was milk meant for Evin. That milk was her last tangible connection to her daughter. She made a ritual out of washing the bottles and tubes and flanges every morning and night.

She measured out the ounces like a scientist in a lab. Matt's doubts about the whole thing were all over his face, but Jillian kept on, even getting up in the middle of the night to pump, imagining when Evin would have awakened, hungry. After just two weeks, their entire freezer was full of bags of breast milk. When Matt said they were running out of room, Jillian bought a used freezer on Craigslist for fifty dollars.

When Jillian did nothing but sleep and pump for the first month, Matt suggested she attend a grief group. He'd found one at the hospital, for women who'd had miscarriages or lost babies.

"I don't want to hear some woman cry about a miscarriage," Jillian said, dabbling in the anger stage of her grief.

"I'm sure there will be women with stories like ours," he said. "Will you just try it?"

Jillian could see he was desperate, worried he might lose her to the same void as he'd lost Evin. So she said, "Fine."

The group was led by a woman named Leah. She was older, in her sixties or seventies. She introduced herself by saying she'd led this group for thirty years. She didn't say if she'd lost a baby herself, and nobody asked.

There were three other women in the group. Kat had had a missed miscarriage, meaning the baby had died around six weeks, but there were no signs of anything being wrong so she didn't find out until her first ultrasound at twelve weeks. "I hate that term—missed miscarriage," Kat had said. "Like I failed to show up for an appointment or something. Like this is my fault."

Alex had recently lost a baby boy in her second trimester. Ben was his name. Alex wondered aloud if she should have chosen to deliver Ben, so she could have held him. Instead, she'd chosen to be put to sleep so he could be surgically removed. She thought of him daily, said her husband wanted to try again and she was terrified. Jillian and Matt hadn't even spoken of trying again.

Briana was thirty weeks pregnant, which made Jillian hate her without even hearing her story. Thirty weeks pregnant was past the point of real danger—such a luxury. Briana could go into labor right then and there and the baby would be fine—small, but fine.

"I was pregnant with twins," Briana explained. "One of the babies died. There was no heartbeat at the twenty-week scan. I know I should be happy about the surviving baby, but I'm just so sad."

She described seeing the dead twin gradually break down and disappear with each ultrasound appointment. Jillian felt guilty for her initial hatred.

Jillian hadn't wanted Matt to be right, but he was—the group was helpful. Every week, on Wednesdays, she showered and got herself dressed a couple hours in advance. It was her one outing of the week. Gradually, that outing led to others—visits to the grocery store, the gym, the movies. Gradually, she returned to some version of her former self.

It was during the fourth or fifth group meeting when Jillian confessed to having hundreds of bags of breast milk in a freezer in her garage.

"It makes total sense to me—the pumping," Leah said. The other women nodded, and Jillian felt a little less weird.

"Maybe you'll get to a point when you'll want to donate it," Leah suggested. "Or maybe you'll just want to keep it for years. Whatever you want to do is fine."

Jillian had never considered what she would do with the breast milk. She just wanted to keep creating it, to keep feeding Evin in some alternate reality. She'd never heard of donating breast milk before.

That night, she went home and googled "donating breast milk" and discovered there were so many women willing to pay exorbitant sums for ounces of what they called "liquid gold." Some of these women couldn't breastfeed themselves because they were taking medications that weren't safe for their babies. Some of them said their milk supply had simply vanished. Some of them had to stop breastfeeding due to recurrent mastitis, infections in their milk ducts making them ill.

Jillian found herself clicking, clicking, clicking, reading about all these women who had healthy babies but were "heartbroken" over their inability to breastfeed. She hated these women, was dumbfounded by their priorities. There was formula, after all. It wasn't like their babies were going to starve. It wasn't like their babies were going to die like hers had.

She was about to close her laptop in a huff when she saw a post from a woman named Sasha.

I've never done anything like this before, but figured I'd give it a shot. My husband and I weren't able to have a baby the old-fashioned way. We tried and lost a few. Five, actually. Then we decided to adopt. We are so grateful for our little one—Caitlin Rose. We've had her home for a few days, and I've been giving her formula. I have no problem with that. She seems happy and healthy. But I know they say, "breast is best, blah blah blah." Of course, I want the best for Caitlin. So here I am. At least when she's older, I can tell her I tried, right?

It was the "blah blah blah" that made Jillian smile. She found herself sending the woman a message.

Hi, Sasha. I have a freezer full of milk in need of a good home. I don't need money for it. I just want it to go to the right person. Congratulations on your baby girl.

Her heart seized as she typed "your baby girl." She swallowed what felt like a huge walnut in her throat. She knew it wasn't rational to keep all the milk for herself. She would save some bags of it, forever, but she didn't need all of it.

The next day, Sasha wrote back. At first, Jillian let Sasha believe that she just had an abundant milk supply, more than she needed. It wasn't until they'd traded several messages that she confessed the truth. Sasha didn't email back; she called (they'd exchanged phone numbers).

"Oh, Jillian," Sasha said.

There was silence. Jillian's lip quivered as she held the phone to her ear.

"I don't know what to say," Sasha said finally.

Somehow, this was better than the platitudes people had lobbed at Matt and Jillian: "Everything happens for a reason," "She's with God now," "You are stronger than you know," "You'll heal in time."

"I just . . . I don't understand life sometimes," Sasha added.

"I know," Jillian said. "Neither do I."

Jillian takes another sip of her still-too-hot tea when there's a lull in her conversation with Sasha. She notices Sasha glance at the ice chest on the chair.

"It's all in there," Jillian says.

Sasha had said she wanted a hundred bags to start—about 400 ounces of milk. She wanted to make sure Caitlin drank it before taking more. She knew how precious it was to Jillian, didn't want Jillian to think a single ounce of it would go to waste.

"I bet she loves it," Sasha says.

"I hope so," Jillian says.

In the birth class Matt and Jillian took, the teacher had mentioned that each mother's breast milk is tailored to her baby's unique needs. The body was smart that way. Jillian wondered if her milk was superpowerful, designed to help an extremely premature baby grow and thrive.

"Matt will be relieved if Caitlin likes it, that's for sure. He can't park in the garage because of the stupid freezer," Jillian says.

"Jerry is so weird about his car. I think he would have a panic attack if he had to park in the driveway," Sasha says.

Jerry is Sasha's husband.

Jillian and Sasha take a moment to pretend that they are just two women joking about their husbands. Then they return to who they really are:

"It's amazing, really, what your body is doing," Sasha says.

Jillian looks down, fiddles with the tag and string of her tea bag.

"It's amazing what it *did*," she says. "I stopped pumping a couple days ago."

When she feels the tears come, she looks up at the ceiling, at the lights, and shakes her head, willing them away.

Sasha reaches across the table, puts her hand on top of Jillian's.

She didn't stop pumping all of a sudden; it was gradual. At first, she stopped getting up in the middle of the night to pump. The exhaustion had caught up with her, and she found herself sleeping twelve-hour stretches, her body no longer on alert, listening for a baby not there. It was like her body had accepted Evin's death before she had.

Her milk supply naturally diminished when the night-pumping stopped. It devastated her at first, seeing less and less milk every day. She sobbed for hours. Matt wrapped his arms around her, held her, tried to sympathize. She knew he didn't understand though. He'd started moving on—working full-time again, playing and coaching soccer again, laughing at TV shows again, cracking a beer with dinner again. But, still, he held her. It was all he could do and all she needed him to do.

Jillian dares to meet Sasha's eyes again and sees liquid pooled in them.

"Now you got me crying," Sasha says.

They both break into smiles and embarrassed laughter.

When they get up to leave, Sasha attempts to pay Jillian, slips cash into her palm, but Jillian won't take it. She shakes her head in adamant refusal.

"I made it for free," she says. "I did it because I wanted to."

Sasha sighs and says, "If you insist. Next time, I'm at least buying you a scone."

They hug again, and it feels right this time, like they are old friends. When they walk out together, Sasha carrying the ice chest, Jillian feels the baristas' eyes on them.

"I bet they think I'm donating a kidney to you or something," Jillian says.

"I read this article about people who want to be vampires. They buy blood from strangers online," Sasha says. "We could be doing that."

Jillian shivers at the thought, says, "People are strange."

They get to Jillian's car first. She gets inside, tells Sasha to text her when Caitlin tries the milk. Sasha says she'll send a photo.

Jillian closes her car door and puts her key in the ignition and then sits a moment, watching Sasha walk away with the ice chest full of milk meant for Evin. In a way, Evin is helping Caitlin grow and thrive. In a way, Evin is living on.

Jillian texts Sasha:

"Don't forget to send me a photo. Hope she likes it."

She adds a crossed-fingers emoji.

Then she texts Matt:

"I survived."

when they were young

WHEN THEY WERE young, idealism gave them the strength to have convictions. They're old now—or old*er* Joe says—and they spend their evenings sitting on their faux leather couch, the dog between them, watching *Jeopardy*. He likes to call out the answers, his volume deliberately increased when Laney is in the kitchen rinsing the dinner dishes or wrapping up the leftovers or is in the bathroom because the beer makes its way through her at around a quarter after seven every night. It's like he's still trying to impress her with his intelligence, just like he did when they were young.

When they were young, they didn't "believe" in television. It was a mind-numbing distraction. They tilted their self-righteous heads and scoffed at those who indulged in such garbage as *Happy Days*, *Knight Rider*, and *Three's Company*. Their recreational reading, their pursuit of real intellectual stimulation via Thoreau and Hemingway was, of course, far superior. They did agree to own one television, for news-gathering purposes, as a daily subscription to the *Los Angeles Times* seemed to be a blatant waste of paper, a contribution to the depletion of the Earth's resources. This one television was to be hidden in a closet or a cabinet. They have three televisions now, all exposed, two perched on dedicated television stands, one bolted to the wall like a work of art. Their younger selves would cringe at their present-day counterparts.

"What is the Bay of Bengal?" Joe shouts as Laney makes her way to the bathroom—7:17 p.m.

They thought a lot of things when they were young. They thought it was arrogant to eat meat, to assume a higher, more privileged position on the food chain. They thought Thanksgiving was a day of mourning, not celebration, because of what the settlers did to the American Indians. They hated Madonna, because everyone else loved her. They didn't see *Back to the Future*, because everyone else did. They thought most people were stupid sheep, waiting to be herded by a media-driven trend. They waxed poetic about the Iran-Contra affair and mulled over Ronald Reagan's politics, while making tofu tacos on Friday nights. They dedicated themselves to raising money to go toward relieving the famine in Ethiopia. They boycotted watching fireworks on the Fourth of July, saying that America had become ethnocentric and willfully ignorant to the problems of the world. Their friends rolled their eyes, but they didn't care. They had each other. Just them against the masses. Them and their lofty ideals and morals and judgments. So high and mighty. So damn above it all. When they were young.

Over the flush of the toilet, Laney hears Joe shout, "What is the Adriatic Sea?" She's been wearing the same that-time-of-the-month underwear since yesterday, in expectation of what has always been predictable. Nothing.

"Laney, you missed it. I swept Bodies of Water," he says.

She resumes her seat on the couch, the far right cushion, indented a bit right of center because she likes to press up against the armrest. The left cushion is Joe's. And Sal (as in Sally), the dog, takes the center, with an occasional ear or paw crossing boundaries.

"I'm sure Sal was impressed," she says.

"She was, weren't you Sal?"

He nuzzles into the dog with affection that makes Laney wonder if he would have hated being a father as much as he'd thought he would.

"Do we really have to go to that thing tomorrow?" he asks.

The *thing* he's referring to is Laney's sister's "welcoming party" for her new baby girl, an Age Zero Birthday Party she's calling it. Sasha's always wanted to be a mother. Since she was a teenager, she's been amassing a collection of baby clothes for her future child—fuzzy jumpers and corduroy overalls and dresses with lace trim. When the collection began, Laney, nearly a decade older than Sasha, told her, "You don't have to be a mother, you know. Women can do all kinds of things now."

Sasha had said, "Why would I want to do anything else?"

After years of trying without success, Sasha and her husband adopted a baby born to a nineteen-year-old. If she wants to throw a little party, Laney can't criticize or even roll her eyes at her enthusiasm. Joe's not related to her directly, and he hasn't seen all the baby clothes she's collected over the years, so he can.

"Of course we have to go."

"It's just going to be all those yuppie moms and their babies, who of course are all going to grow up to be senators, astronauts, and Olympians and—"

"We're leaving at noon," Laney says.

"How long do we have to stay?"

The final *Jeopardy* category is revealed—Astronomy. Joe can't even find the Big Dipper on a perfectly clear night.

"She's my only sister," Laney says and leaves her cushion.

They had known each other only a handful of months when Joe said, without hesitation or prefacing, "Do you want kids?"

It was at Stoney Point, at the trailhead. Every Sunday, they hiked to the top of what looked like a big pile of rocks God had thrown down during a divine version of Legos. They'd sit, look at the valley below, eat apples, and "get stoney," as they liked to say.

Just a moment before he asked the question, a girl around

five or six years old had skipped past them, shrieking with glee as her father chased after her, growling playfully like a grizzly bear. It was as if that one simple scene gave birth to Joe's question, as if he'd never before considered children. Women are raised to believe fully in maternity-as-destiny. Laney's own mother gave her plastic dolls with accompanying miniature bottles that could actually be filled with liquid when she was just a child herself. Motherhood was the social norm. When they were young, the norm repulsed them.

"Do I want kids? Hmm . . . I don't think so," Laney said.

"Me neither," he said, walking ahead with a shrug, as if they'd just agreed they didn't feel like lasagna for dinner.

"It seems selfish," Laney said.

"Selfish. Exactly. I mean who could bring a kid into this world?"

She was right on his heels, careful not to step on the back of his hiking boots, so worn that kicked-up granules of dirt found their way into the cracks where the sole had pulled away from the shoe.

"I guess most people don't really think about it," she said.

"Well, we think."

The superiority in his tone made her feel important.

"I'm just afraid I'd resent it," she said, keeping her hypothetical baby genderless and distant.

"You probably would," he said. "We're driven people, Laney. We have ambitions. We're going to do something with our lives."

They didn't know what, exactly, they were going to do, but something. Currently, Laney manages a specialty grocery store that stocks things like bacon jam and teriyaki seaweed chips. Joe sits in a cubicle and proofreads air-conditioning manuals. They sublet an apartment in Arcadia that Joe insists is more like a town house.

"A kid would be a distraction. We'd regret it," he'd said.

Laney was taken aback by the "we," by the suggestion that their relationship would last long enough for them to unite and make such a lifelong decision. He was the first boyfriend she'd had for more than a few weeks.

"You're probably right," she said.

He readjusted the straps on his backpack and continued hiking.

"Are we awful?" she asked.

"No, we're wise," he said, with an authority that made him sexy and powerful and inspiring and made her sexy and powerful and inspiring by association. Yes, they were wise. They were realists. They recognized the sacrifices of parenthood. They verbalized truths that all those reluctant, and now-agonized, parents never did. They were enlightened. They were lucky. They were sure to be happy. When they were young.

·◦·

There are two pink balloons tied to the mailbox, and a multitude of minivans (and the types of ridiculously sized

SUVs that Joe will criticize) are parked on the street. They park behind an Expedition with a license plate frame that reads "Triplets . . . Outnumbered from Day 1."

"They own impractical gas guzzlers, and they're reproducing with reckless abandon," Joe says.

She would have welcomed this invitation to judge, carried on his rant, when they were young. Now she asks, "Did you sign the card?"

The front door is open, so they walk in, Laney leading the way, Joe following with his hands stuffed into the front pockets of his jeans. They're the same jeans he was wearing earlier while working on the Mustang. It's leaking enough oil in the carport for the landlord to leave a handwritten note on their door. Laney told Joe they should just sell the thing, that people will pay good money for a '70 Mustang because of the nostalgia and all that. They could use the money for a trip somewhere. He says she's too practical.

Sasha is across the room, talking and nodding and smiling with various women Laney's never seen before. Sasha's always been the social one. The youngest siblings usually are. Joe and Laney don't have many friends. They don't throw dinner parties or invite couples over to play Cranium. They have their weekly conversations with the regulars at the dog park. Bill and Wendy are around the same age. Deb and Marco don't come around as much anymore, ever since Marco's ALS put him in a wheelchair. "I feel bad for Deb," Laney had told Joe. Joe had replied with his standard insensitivity: "Seriously. He's basically an invalid."

Sasha looks relaxed, her curly hair swept up into a loose and messy bun. Not that it's possible to tell from a few minutes of across-the-room analysis, but she seems happy. It's something in her posture, the way her hands rest comfortably on her hips. Their mother used to joke that Sasha got the childbearing ones. It wasn't funny all those years she couldn't sustain a pregnancy. One miscarriage after another, no medical explanation.

Laney leaves Joe in the foyer (because Sasha lives in a house that has such a thing) and makes her way through the chatter of soon-to-be and new mothers, picking up on terms like "breast pump" and "sleep regression." Sasha is talking to a woman who is holding a glass of sparkling cider by the stem with just two dainty fingers. This woman says, "I really think God made the gestation period ten months so there would be time to go through all the insanity and reach sanity again." They laugh.

"Hey, Sash," Laney says.

"Elaine," she says, wrapping her arms around Laney's middle. "I'm so glad you came. Where's Joe?"

Laney points to him, standing by the gift table like he's a security officer protecting the wrapped onesies.

"Elaine, this is my good friend, Blanca. She also just had a baby. Three days before Caitlin."

It's no secret that Sasha did not actually give birth, but she speaks as if it is.

"Wow, congratulations."

"Are your kids here?" Blanca asks Laney.

The silence sets in, the awkward kind. It happens every time they come to an event like this. Laney can't blame Joe for patrolling the gift table.

"Oh, Elaine doesn't have kids," Sasha says.

Blanca's brows furrow, and she says, "I'm sorry."

"No, she doesn't *want* them," Sasha adds hurriedly, with a nervous laugh, as if it's funny. It wasn't funny all those years Sasha couldn't have a child. Laney's choice seemed to deeply offend her.

"Elaine likes her personal time," Sasha explains. She always feels this need to explain.

"Oh, well. Can't say I blame you. I feel like I'll never sleep eight hours straight again," Blanca says.

"Same," Sasha says. And they bond. And imply that Laney is the odd one because she is accustomed to a full night of usually restful sleep.

When they were young, Laney and Joe watched their couple friends convert into families, as one belly after another popped out into that strange oblong shape. They could maintain some sort of denial-based social circle as long as the belly was all they had to contend with. They even participated in baby name conversations, delighted in offering suggestions like "Thelonious" and "Geraldine," just for the hell of it.

But when the babies arrived, along with the invitations to christenings and baptisms, it was all too obvious that they were perpetuating a past and that everyone else their age had propelled themselves into the future. They went to one birthday party, with a clown and a cake made mostly of pink frosting, then began to RSVP "no" when they received the dinosaur- or ballerina-themed invitations, then just stopped opening the cards, left them with the other throwaway promotional mail promising low interest rates on something unnecessary. It really was just them against the masses. They couldn't relate. They didn't want any of it—the diapers, the crying fits, the dressing and feeding and caring for them while they puked or sneezed or sweated out a 104-degree fever. They didn't want the temper tantrums, the whining for plastic toys-of-the-moment that they'd discard after two weeks. They didn't want the broken bones and runny noses and chicken pox. They didn't want the worry. They didn't want to stop calling each other "babe" and start referring to each other as the child would—"go tell Daddy that Mommy says dinner's ready."

"I feel like they judge us because we're not like them," Laney had said to him once.

He'd shrugged. "How could it possibly be wrong for me to want to give all my love to only you?"

He was right—how could that be wrong?

They had this fantasy of mutual absorption, of making wishes on each other's stray eyelashes, of spending eternity discovering each other's every crevice, every nook and cranny. They'd be as intimate as two humans could be. They'd fart and laugh together. They'd make love every night, sometimes fuck, and always hold each other afterward. They'd read in bed, attentive to their own respective books, their feet kneading against each other. They'd give each other massages and spoon at night. They'd take bubble baths in an old-fashioned tub with claw feet. They'd drink beer—or, better yet, they'd brew their own in their garage. They'd search for recipes, exotic ones, requiring special trips to exotic grocery stores where cashiers would speak very broken English. They'd have an old house, one with character, with wood paneling instead of suburbia stucco. And there would be a wraparound porch. They'd grow their own marijuana in their own yard— they'd have a yard!—and smoke joints under the stars. They'd have a telescope, to look at those stars and quiz each other on the names of constellations. They'd have a classic car to cruise around in on weekends. It would be polished, and the tires would be shiny black. They'd camp in Yosemite and go to Italy one summer. They'd always wanted to go to Oaxaca for Día de los Muertos, so they'd go. They'd just *go*. They'd do that coast trip, drive all the way to Canada, stopping every half hour to take pictures. They'd have a few dogs and a few cats, just roaming around freely. These pets would have creative names—no human names or typical, standard-issue names that kids come up with, like Spot. They'd go to the Dresden, frequent jazz bars, see movies. On weeknights!

They'd buy good furniture, or bad furniture because they'd have the time and money to refurbish it. They'd subscribe to magazines. They'd have plants on windowsills. They'd grow herbs and vegetables. In their garden! They'd have a bird feeder and recognize the frequent visitors. They'd have all sorts of saucepans for cooking. They'd have a fireplace with real logs that crackle. They'd run 5Ks and ride bikes and find hiking trails. They'd get season tickets to the Hollywood Bowl and bring a picnic basket with things like bruschetta in it. They'd go to baseball games, visit every stadium in the country, and have soft pretzels and chocolate malts with the little wooden tongue-depressor-like spoons. They'd read at coffee shops on Sunday mornings, play board games for hours, wander in used bookstores, walk along the beach at night, go to museums and exhibits and discuss them. They'd know something about art. They'd go out to eat whenever they wanted and order appetizers and soups of the day and desserts. They'd take a dance class. They'd bake. They'd go to farmers markets. They'd have votive candles, always lit. They'd buy old records, just to have them. They'd wrinkle together and love every moment of it.

Joe has begun to take gifts from people arriving, arranging the boxes and bags on the table with a system known only to him.

"Are you just going to stand here all day?" Laney asks him.

"Who says we're going to be here all day?"

"We haven't even seen the baby yet."

"Well, where is she?"

Sasha's husband, Jerry, is not an attractive man. He is maybe five foot six on a good day, and his hair is receding from his forehead, leaving a cul-de-sac of baldness. Despite these conventionally unappealing traits, he is surrounded by eight women.

"I think Jerry has her," Laney says, taking Joe by the wrist and leading him into the living room.

Sure enough, baby Caitlin is lying in Jerry's arms, her head on one forearm, legs on the other. Everyone is calling her "precious."

Laney and Joe stand behind Jerry, peeking over his shoulders to see what is compelling these seemingly sane adults to make googly eyes and contort their faces. She looks like a doll, something right off a shelf in a collector's store. Her brown eyes are huge—not typical, squinty newborn eyes. And she has a full head of black hair. They've combed it to the side and used a tiny barrette to hold a strand in place above her ear. They have dressed her in a lavender dress and put ruffle socks on her feet, but she lies peacefully, unaware of the fuss.

"Hello there, Caitlin," Laney says in a cutesy voice she's never heard herself produce. Out of the corner of her eye, she can see Joe watching her watch Caitlin, and there's this surprise on his face. After being with someone a few decades, surprise is rare.

Jerry turns around and says, "Elaine! Joe!" He's the type to say everything with an exclamation point.

Caitlin does nothing more than twitch her nose during the bustle of her father rising from his seat and pushing past the female onlookers to greet Laney and Joe.

"Thanks for coming, guys. How are you?"

"We're good," Joe says, shifting his weight to his heels.

"She's really beautiful," Laney says, with a sincerity that probably also surprises Joe. On the way over, she'd thought she would have to say something like that, in an obligatory way, even if the baby had red blotches on her face and a yellow jaundiced tint to her skin.

"Want to hold her?"

Before Laney has a chance to answer, Jerry is presenting his new daughter like a pot roast on a platter.

In the transfer, the baby sneezes, but she quickly assumes Laney's forearm as her new pillow. Laney feels like she should sit, like standing is too risky for this baby-holding responsibility. She takes slow steps backward until she finds a plastic folding chair against the wall and lowers herself into it. Joe could have brought the chair to her once he saw her intention to find it, but it's as if he's playing that childhood game of standing on a kitchen tile, pretending all else around that tile is dangerous quicksand.

The baby's head is heavier than Laney thought it would be. Jerry keeps telling her to "just relax" and "make sure to support her head," which makes her think she's not doing her job properly, like she's causing the baby discomfort, straining her little neck muscles. Her concern with Caitlin's neck muscles alarms her.

She really is beautiful. Laney fixates on her eyelashes and feels a sadness weigh on her insides. She's felt it before. It happens every time the Girl Scouts arrive on their doorstep, with red wagons full of cookies. There's usually one girl with a sock slouched down around her ankle or a pigtail that is horribly out of line with the other, and it just makes her heart ache. She's felt it when the kids come around in their costumes at Halloween and deliver the latest version of verbal kid excitement—"Rad!" or "Cool!" or "Dope!"—when she drops one of the big, adult-sized Snickers bars into their pillowcases and plastic pumpkin pails. Last year, Joe wanted to just leave out a bowl of the bite-sized versions and go to a movie, to avoid "the hassle." That made her heart ache too. And it always catches her off guard during back-to-school time, when the kids are begging their parents in the aisles of Walmarts for lunch boxes with a trendy action figure on them. The squeals that come out of these kids, as if their lives depend on packing their lunch in something cool (or rad, or dope), are annoying to the ears but somehow tenderly amusing. It's like seeing children reminds her that priorities are all relative and arbitrary. Joe used to say that children were mere distraction from each other and from what is truly important in life. But maybe love, life, and sanity are dependent on occasional distraction.

"Her hands are so tiny," Laney says, marveling at the nails so perfectly in place, comparing them to her own, finding it unbelievable that she used to be this small and that Caitlin will someday be her size.

"She's a baby," Joe says, with a laugh and a glance at Jerry, maybe hoping that he, as a male, will laugh too, or possibly wink to suggest he agrees that the baby marveling is nonsense. The baby burps though, so delicately, as if she was born with manners, and Jerry is busy tending to her, dabbing her mouth with the blanket from his shoulder.

"I'll take her back from you in a second. It's almost time for her milk," Jerry says in a baby voice.

Laney doesn't even have to look at Joe to know his eyes are rolling. The other day, Laney had told him that Sasha was getting breast milk from a woman she met on the internet, and Joe was beside himself. Laney thought it was a bit ridiculous too, but Joe's response made her want to defend Sasha: "She just wants the best for her child, Joe."

"I'm going to get some food," Joe says, retreating to the kitchen.

He hovers over the cheese and crackers, taking his time, like he just can't decide what he wants. He takes a Ritz with a slice of cheddar and eats it, in three bites, when he could have just put the whole damn thing in his mouth, like he usually would. Then he takes another Ritz and nibbles on that one. And, suddenly, Laney wants to cover Caitlin's ears and tell Jerry (whom she has had maybe half a conversation with in her life) everything she hates about Joe.

How he thinks he's so easygoing but does things like insist on putting the toilet paper roll on so that the paper pulls from the bottom.

How he refuses to get gas until the empty light comes on.

How he gets food out of his teeth by employing this sucking mechanism with his tongue.

How he puts his gum on the side of his plate before a meal and resumes chewing it after.

How he clips his toenails while sitting on the toilet and leaves them on the bathroom floor, so that they inevitably stick to the bottoms of her feet when she steps out of the shower.

How he clears the phlegm in his throat and swallows it.

How he pours full glasses of juice, drinks half, and then forgets about them.

How he cusses and swears about how inconsiderate people are when he gets cut off on the freeway but then proceeds to cut off other people, claiming he is an "assertive driver."

How when they pass by a nice restaurant Laney mentions wanting to try, the type of restaurant with a fish tank the size of a wall and expensive chandeliers and gold-plated napkin rings, he has to feed her his diatribe about the disgusting extravagance of Americans (as if he isn't one) who ignore the starving people in Africa. *Yes, Joe, you are a better, more advanced human being than all of us.*

How, in all their years together, he's taken her to only a handful of movies on weeknights, most of which have not been "date-like." The last one was the latest *Star Wars* movie, which they saw to pass time while the mechanic did their oil change. It was the Tuesday special—lube, oil, filter, plus tire rotation and seven-point inspection for $26.99.

"Elaine, are you okay?" Jerry asks.

It's only when she rolls up her eyes to tell him she's fine that she realizes a tear is running down her cheek.

"I'm fine," she says, heat filling her face, burning her cheeks from the inside out.

"Are you sure?" he asks, reaching for Caitlin.

Laney gives the baby to him and excuses herself to the bathroom. Joe calls after her, concern in his voice: "Laney?"

She splashes cold water on her face and leaves the faucet on while she sits on the toilet, threadbare underwear around her ankles. Every twenty-eight days usually, like clockwork, as they say. The doctor said it would stop, said it stops for most women by her age. But still.

"Laney? What's going on? You okay?" Joe says.

"Leave me alone. I'm fine."

"You sure?"

She gets up off the toilet and closes her eyes while her head spins. The doctor also said dizziness may accompany the hot flashes.

How has time gone so quickly? How is she *old*? There were so many choices she took for granted—the choice to have a child, for one. It's not that she wanted a child—did she? She doesn't know anymore. Really, it's the choice she mourns. Pondering something like a child is a luxury of the young. So much is a luxury of the young. And the young are too shortsighted to appreciate this. On the subject of regret and long-lost dreams, people say, "It's never too late." But, sometimes, it is. Sometimes time passes, and it is too late.

She opens the door a crack, just enough for Joe to see her face, moist with tears and sweat beads. He looks genuinely worried.

"What's wrong, babe?"

Babe. They still call each other that. They may not have been to Oaxaca (yet, Joe would say), and they may take baths in a too-shallow tub without claw feet, and their "garden" may be a patch of yellowed grass to the left of their front door—but he still calls her babe.

"I'm fine," she says, feeling the heat leave her, simmering down through her body, exiting through her toes.

"You don't look fine," he says, using the knuckle of his index finger to wipe the snot from underneath her nose.

"It's just that I . . . I haven't gotten my period," she says, lip quivering.

When they were young, that was the dreaded announcement.

He looks stunned; his face goes white.

"What?" he says. His voice cracks. "What do you mean? Are you sure?"

She smiles gently and leans in to kiss his nose. Poor Joe. He just doesn't realize they're not young anymore.

only in Hollywood

EVERY MOTHER'S DAY for the past few decades, Leah has taken herself to see the saddest movie she can find. This year, it's a movie called *Mothers and Daughters*. The title alone is enough to make her cry.

It's not always easy to find a sad movie in May. Most of the dramas come out in late fall or early winter, primed for Oscar season. Over the years, she's had to go to second-run theaters to find tearjerkers. She's usually the only one in the theater, sitting in the back with a box of Kleenex. Some favorites of Mother's Days past: *Sophie's Choice*, *Dead Man Walking*, *Titanic*, *Million Dollar Baby*.

The movie that stays with her is *Losing Isaiah*. Halle Berry plays a crack cocaine addict who leaves her baby in a dumpster, promising to "come back later." The baby is found and adopted into a loving family. A few years later, Halle Berry's character completes rehab and tells her caseworker about abandoning her baby. The caseworker investigates, a legal battle ensues, and Isaiah is reunited with his birth mother.

When Leah saw the movie, she couldn't help but look around the theater, self-conscious, thinking it must be obvious that this story was about her. There were differences, of course. Leah hadn't been a crack addict. Her baby was a girl. And Leah hadn't told her she'd come back later.

Leah's parents had a strict rule about dating: not before the age of eighteen, and never a non-Jew. So when Thomas Barrett stopped by the deli where Leah worked and asked her on a date, she knew saying yes would mean telling her parents myriad lies, which, if discovered, could result in her being sent away to the Jewish boarding school that was often mentioned as a threat.

She said yes anyway. Because it was Thomas Barrett, a senior, the boy in school all the girls liked. And she was just Leah Dollmann, a sophomore, a nobody.

For that first date, she told her parents she was spending the night at Rachel Cohen's house. They liked Rachel, knew her parents from Temple. Rachel had agreed, reluctantly, to be the alibi. She was as worried about getting in trouble as Leah. They both feared their parents, their always-serious parents who saw the worst in everything and everyone. It was a generational thing. If you'd escaped the Holocaust, you had no hope of seeing anything else.

Technically, she *would* be spending the night at Rachel's—that was the plan. She was just going to a movie with Thomas first. She wasn't really lying; she was just withholding some information. That's what she told herself.

They decided to see *One Hundred and One Dalmatians* at the Olympic Drive-In. Leah figured if she did get caught, she would tell her parents she'd just gone to see a Disney movie. What could be more innocent than that?

Thomas picked her up in front of the grocery store on Thornton Avenue. That was their planned rendezvous point. It all felt so exciting, getting into the passenger's seat of his blue Chevy Bel Air. Leah had never been on a real date before. She'd danced with boys at bar and bat mitzvahs. That was the extent of her romantic experience. She still didn't understand why Thomas wanted to go out with her. Rachel said it was because she was the prettiest sophomore. But Leah, like many fifteen-year-old girls, couldn't see herself as pretty.

They shared a bag of popcorn during the movie, their hands touching when they both reached in at the same time. Just that, the smallest contact, made Leah's whole body warm. She wondered if Thomas would kiss her when he dropped her off. She smiled at the thought of Rachel's awestruck face upon hearing the story. Neither of them would be able to sleep.

What happened, though, was not something she would tell Rachel, or anyone else for that matter.

The plan was for Thomas to drop off Leah at the park near Rachel's house. Leah couldn't risk him pulling up at Rachel's house; her parents might see. There was a brightly lit lot at the park, but he didn't stop there. He parked at the dark end of the street, near the basketball courts. Something about his face, illuminated just barely by an overhead streetlight, made her nervous. He looked like someone telling ghost stories around a campfire.

He slid over on the seat, closer to her. His car had just the one bench seat in front, no center console, no barrier to be crossed. When his hip touched hers, he put his hand on her knee. She was wearing a blue shirtwaist dress from Montgomery Ward, a dress her mother had bought her to wear to her cousin's upcoming Bat Mitzvah. She felt shy about her bared knees, unsure what to do about his hand lingering there. She shifted in her seat as his hand inched slowly up her leg.

When she started to say something, he put his mouth on hers. It wasn't the sweet kiss she'd imagined. It was wet and sloppy and forceful. He stuck his tongue in her mouth, moved it around like he was cleaning her teeth. Her instinct was to lean away, to press her palms into his chest. But she was no match for his persistence. Before she knew it, his body was on top of hers, pinning her down, her head pressed up against the door handle.

"Have you done this before?" he whispered into her ear. His breath was hot.

She didn't know what "this" was, so she didn't say anything.

"The guys said you'd be difficult," he said.

It wasn't until after it was all over, after he'd left her there at that park, where she cried for an hour before walking to Rachel's house, that she understood—she'd been a bet.

He didn't take off her dress; he just pushed it up around her waist. Then he unzipped his pants and put himself inside her. It was only when he shushed her that she realized she'd yelped.

She closed her eyes tightly, but the tears still escaped. When he was done, after what must have been a couple minutes but felt like hours, she felt the wetness on her cheeks and between her legs. He pushed himself off her and slid over to the driver's seat, zipping up the fly of his pants as he turned the key in the ignition.

She pushed herself up slowly, put her fingers where he'd been, saw they were red. He looked at her fingers and said, "It was your first time, huh?"

Leah still wasn't entirely sure what had happened. This would sound strange to a fifteen-year-old girl today. Today, kids in elementary school know about sex. In 1961, Leah knew next to nothing. Back then, sex ed was comically vague. Leah's teacher, Mrs. Clancy, talked about how plants reproduced, showing diagrams, expecting that the students would read between the lines and figure it out. The only fact Leah knew about sex was that it was something that happened when you got married.

Her mother said the same thing about babies—"You have

to be married to have a baby." So when Leah missed her period, she didn't think she could be pregnant because she wasn't married. About a month after what happened with Thomas, she started feeling sick. When she threw up her breakfast one morning, her father said, "You must have that flu going around," and she thought, *Yes, I must.*

Years later, Leah would look back on all this and be in awe of her denial. A part of her had to have known what was happening but refused to allow the soft whisper of truth to become audible in her mind. Months in, when her clothes became snug, she started holding her skirts together with pins. She wore tent-like dresses that didn't cinch at the waist. She pretended that everything was fine, as if she were just a normal high-school girl. But, of course, this deception could go on for only so long.

It was at the breakfast table, after her father had gone to work, that Leah's mother said, "Wait," as Leah got up to take her cereal bowl to the sink.

She turned around and looked at her mother.

"Do you think I am a fool?" her mother said in Yiddish. She used Yiddish only when she was too angry, too flummoxed to remember the correct English.

"What is it, Mama? I don't know what you mean," Leah said.

"You're *expecting*. I can see it."

Back then, the word "pregnant" was almost considered crass. Leah's mother couldn't bear saying it. She stared at

Leah's belly. Leah looked down, saw what she saw, the slight roundness beginning to take shape.

"You are lucky your father didn't notice first," her mother spat.

"I'm not . . . *expecting*. I don't know what you mean," Leah said, believing her lies, or wanting to. She started to cry.

"Who is the boy?" her mother said.

Leah knew then that this had to do with Thomas. He'd had sex with her, and she was pregnant. She thought of Karen and Alter, the owners of the deli where she'd been working since the previous summer. She had heard them having an argument just the week before, in the small office next to the bathroom. Karen had been crying, saying how she didn't understand why it was so easy for some women to get pregnant while she could not. Alter was trying to calm her down, and she was getting angry at him. Leah eavesdropped longer than she should have. She stopped only when she heard the bell chime, meaning someone had come in the front door. She ran back to the counter, her heart racing.

Her mother repeated the question: "Who is the boy?"

Leah just said, "I don't know."

There was so much she didn't know.

It was obvious Leah's mother had told her father when he stopped looking Leah in the eye. She'd been scared of him screaming, maybe even hitting her, but his silence was much worse. It was as if she no longer existed to him. Her mother wasn't talking much to her either, but she still looked her in the eye, always with disgust.

School was out for summer, so Leah's parents told everyone that Leah had gone to visit relatives in Northern California, relatives that did not exist. The truth was that Leah was at home, ordered to stay inside. "We can't have anyone seeing you like this," her mother said. Leah had to quit her job at the deli. She wasn't allowed to see Rachel. She couldn't open the front door for the postman. She couldn't even go to Temple.

Two weeks before school was to start, Leah's parents came into her bedroom, where she was reading *Charlotte's Web* for the twentieth time that summer, the book resting on her belly.

"You need to pack a bag of clothes. We are leaving in the morning," her mother said.

"Be ready at six o'clock," her father added. It was the first thing he'd said to her in months.

The next morning, they drove in silence for nearly an hour. Leah didn't know where they were going. They pulled off the highway near Pasadena and, after several turns on side streets, stopped in front of what looked like an old mansion in the English countryside. There were big trees and a winding drive, ending in front of a huge staircase that led to thick, double front doors. Leah's parents got out of the car, so she did the same. She followed them up the staircase, slouched behind her father as he knocked on the door.

It was only when they got inside that Leah started to understand where she was. There were other girls there, girls who were *expecting*. They all looked sad. A woman named Esther introduced herself as the owner of Fleischer Home then gave them a tour.

Leah followed behind her parents and Esther on the tour. She felt sick. The toast with jam she'd had for breakfast seemed to be coming up from her stomach. She kept swallowing, trying to keep it down.

There was dark woodwork everywhere—railings, built-in cabinets, three flights of creaky stairs. The home allowed twenty-two girls at a time. Leah would share a room with one other girl. She'd have her own twin bed and a dresser. There was a big meal room, where some girls were having breakfast. Esther mentioned that they gave the girls water pills every day so they wouldn't retain water. She also said that nobody used their real name. "You'll want to think of your new name, okay?" she said to Leah, presenting this requirement as a fun game.

When her parents left, Leah felt instant loneliness, an abandonment she'd never experienced before. They didn't hug her or kiss her cheek before they left. They just thanked Esther and told Leah they would pick her up in a few months, after the baby's birth. It was always "the baby," never "your baby." It was always a "situation," a problem to be solved. Leah was starting to understand—her parents wanted her to hide here, at this house with other pregnant girls then have the baby and return to school as if nothing had happened.

For the first few days, Leah's body felt too heavy to move. She just lay in bed, staring at the ceiling. She'd never been away from home like this before. She'd had one-night sleepovers with Rachel occasionally, but that was it. She missed her parents, even though they'd barely spoken to her since they'd found out. She missed her bedroom at home, her books, her things. She missed Rachel, wondered if Rachel was suspicious of Leah's supposed trip to visit relatives she'd never mentioned before. What would her friends think when school started and Leah wasn't there? Would they talk about her?

She knew she wasn't the only one who was lonely and sad. She heard other girls crying in their rooms, almost every night. Leah found some solace in these other girls. Her roommate was a fourteen-year-old who went by "Carol," though her real name was Abigail, Abby for short. Leah came to learn that real names were disclosed right away among the girls; this idea of protecting their identities was a ruse for their parents' benefit. Leah's best friend in the home became Miriam (who went by "Mary"). She had long strawberry blonde hair and Ben Franklin glasses. She was smart, seemingly smart enough to have avoided this predicament in the first place.

"My boyfriend told me he was pulling out," she said when they first met each other. Most first conversations involved an exchange of two things: your real name and how you got pregnant. Miriam was seventeen, due in November, a month before Leah.

The hospital was just a block away from the home. If someone said, "Oh, she went over," that meant a girl went to the hospital to give birth. A few days later, the girl would come back. She would usually stay another week or so at the home to recover. She always looked older, changed. The other girls would crowd around, asking what it was like. Esther and the staff didn't like when the girls talked like this, but they couldn't prevent it either. Sometimes they told everyone to go to their rooms when conversations of certain birth stories became too graphic. They didn't want the girls to be scared.

"A couple weeks before you came, this one girl threw herself down the stairs, trying to kill her baby, because she didn't want to go into labor. She just wanted to go back to school, go on with her life," Miriam told Leah. "I don't think she understood that you have to *deliver* the baby, whether it's dead or not."

Leah didn't know this, but she pretended she did.

"And I've heard of girls who have run away," Miriam said.

"Where do they go?" Leah asked.

Miriam shrugged. "Maybe back to their boyfriends. Maybe they just move away and start brand-new lives with their babies. That's what I like to think."

It wasn't all bad. They went out on weekends, usually to the movies or a park or an ice cream parlor. The girls all wore fake wedding rings, though it had to be obvious what their situations were—a bunch of pregnant teenagers just walking around together. The lead cook, Bea, used to refer to them as "a bunch of marshmallows on toothpicks." Most of the girls were visited by their parents on Sunday. Some girls came from other states, their parents desperate to ensure their desecrated daughters wouldn't be recognized somewhere. Those girls didn't get visits. Leah didn't either. She was embarrassed to admit that it wasn't because her parents lived far away; they just couldn't stand the sight of her.

There was a roster on the bulletin board by the staircase with everyone's chores—washing dishes, cleaning the toilets, running the vacuum, helping in the kitchen, setting the table, those kinds of things. When new girls came, their names would go to the bottom of the list. As Leah's name moved up, she knew she was getting closer to delivering. She still didn't know what that would entail and was grateful that Miriam would go first.

Miriam's water broke two weeks before her due date. It was in the middle of the night. Leah hadn't heard the commotion. When she woke up the next morning, Abby told her: "Miriam went over last night." Later that evening, they got word that she'd had her baby—a girl.

Miriam returned to the home a few days later. She looked tired, her hair gathered in a messy bun on top of her head, a loose shirt hanging over her now deflated body. She gave everyone a smile, but Leah knew it was forced, fake. When they were finally alone, sitting on Leah's bed while Abby was in the meal room eating lunch, Miriam broke down.

"Oh god, Leah, it was awful," she said.

It wasn't the pain that had been awful, though it was; it was being alone through it. She was completely knocked out during the delivery—the norm back then. When she woke up, she didn't remember anything. She just saw a nurse at her bedside, changing a sanitary napkin, and said, "What happened?" The nurse said, "You had your baby."

They wouldn't let her see the baby until the next day.

"She was so sweet, Leah. She cuddled up against my neck, like a kitten nuzzling. I counted her toes, just like everyone says you do."

Leah felt her own tears come as she saw Miriam's filling her eyes.

"On the third day, I knew I'd have to say goodbye. I tried to tell myself to be okay about it. They said the baby would go to a good home. They had me sign these forms. It was all so fast. And then the nurse came and got her, and all I remember is her little pink blanket. I could see it over the nurse's shoulder as she walked out."

Miriam started sobbing, and Leah pulled her close, so close that she could feel her chest heaving up and down against her own.

"I mean, I did the right thing, didn't I?" Miriam pleaded.

The message they repeated over and over at the home was that adoption was "best for the baby." They led the girls to believe that all of their babies would be adopted into families with husbands who were doctors and housewives committed to crafts and cooking and creating the very best life possible for their child. The girls were told, in no uncertain terms, that they were not fit to be mothers themselves. It wasn't even discussed as an option.

"You did the right thing," Leah said, trying to sound convincing.

Miriam collapsed into Leah, lay her head in Leah's lap.

"Just, whatever you do, don't get attached," Miriam told Leah.

A moment later, she sat up, with urgency, and said, "Or run away. Keep the baby."

"I can't do that," Leah said. "My parents would—"

"I know," Miriam interrupted. She collapsed into Leah's lap again. "I know."

Five weeks later, Leah had just gotten into bed for the night when her contractions started. She didn't know that's what they were at first. She'd heard of other girls having "false alarm" pains, and she assumed that's what these were. She tried to sleep, but they kept getting worse. She told herself not to worry—after all, her water hadn't broken. A few hours into this, she was sweating and having difficulty not moaning.

"Are you okay?" Abby asked.

In the darkness of their room, Leah could see Abby sit

up in bed, resting on her elbows, her giant belly protruding. Abigail was due a week after Leah.

"I don't know," Leah said.

In between the pains, she felt perfectly fine. Then they would return and she would feel like someone was taking her insides and twisting them, as if wringing out a wet towel.

"It's happening," Abby said, not as a question, but a statement.

The hospital was as lonesome as Miriam had described. Leah's labor was long—twenty-seven hours—so when the first nurse's shift ended, she hoped the next nurse on duty would be nicer. But no. They were all cold, indifferent to her pain. She could hear the judgment in their condescending tone. When they ordered her to "turn over" or "roll over," what she heard was *tramp, whore*. They didn't explain what they were doing, they just did it—inserted the enema, shaved her pubic area. She wished her mother were there. She wondered if the Home had called her parents, told them what was happening. She wondered if her parents cared, or if they just wanted to know when the baby was officially gone.

She was woozy when she woke up after delivery. Miriam had warned her about this. Miriam had also told her not to expect to see her own baby, but Leah had to ask anyway.

"Can I see the baby?" She resorted to "the baby" instead of "my baby," in accordance with the approved language.

The nurse was making notes on a clipboard across the room. She looked up at Leah's question.

"In a few hours, we will bring the baby," she said.

"Is it a girl?" Leah asked.

She'd thought all along that she was having a girl. She had already picked out the baby's name, secretly. She'd tried hard not to fantasize about such things, but she couldn't help it.

"Yes, a girl," the nurse said, looking down at her paperwork again.

The name she'd chosen was Elizabeth. She'd always loved that name, used to give her dolls that name.

"Is she okay? The baby?" Leah asked.

The nurse just said "Mm-hmm" and left.

They brought Elizabeth to her that afternoon. She was wrapped snugly in a pink blanket. Her eyes were closed. She had the longest lashes. And the cutest nose. And the most perfect lips—with a tiny Cupid's bow on the top lip. Leah touched her cheek with a tentative finger, and the baby opened her eyes. They were a dark blue, like the middle of the ocean. She had a full head of dark hair, almost black, like Leah's. Leah thought, "I can't wait to see if it grows in curly like mine," and then she remembered that she wouldn't get to know such a thing.

"Ten minutes, okay?" the nurse said, giving Leah the look

a kindergarten teacher gives a misbehaving five-year-old.

Leah nodded, feigning agreement while she panicked inside.

It all became so clear and urgent:

She couldn't leave the hospital without this baby.

She couldn't give this baby to *strangers*.

When she swung her legs over the side of the bed and stood, she felt light-headed. She held the baby to her chest, closely. She'd come into the hospital with just a small overnight bag. The Home had given them all a list of items to pack in their bags. The packing of the bag at thirty-six weeks pregnant was something of a ritual.

Leah held the baby in the crook of one arm while she pawed through her bag with her free hand. She took out a dress, the dress she'd worn when she arrived at the hospital, and her shoes, a worn pair of beige espadrilles. She set the baby on the bed while she changed, quickly, aware that the nurse had said she was coming back in just ten minutes.

"Thank you, sweet girl," she whispered to Elizabeth, grateful for her silence. Part of Leah thought Elizabeth's silence was condoning her actions; if she wasn't meant to leave with her, the baby would protest.

She went back to her bag and repositioned the clothes within to make something of a bed for the baby. While she shuffled things around, she found a piece of paper, folded, tucked into one of the inside pockets. She unfolded it and read.

Dear Leah,

If you're reading this, you've probably had your baby. I hope you are OK.

I'm moving in with a girlfriend when I'm out of here.

Please call me there if you need anything at all.

Love,
Miriam
213-555-3829

Leah stuffed the note into the pocket of her dress then placed the baby into the bag. As she zipped it, she whispered, "I'm sorry, Elizabeth. It will just be for a few minutes."

It was the first time she'd said her daughter's name out loud.

She opened the door to her room and peered out into the hallway. There was a patient in a wheelchair and a couple nurses, but everyone seemed to be preoccupied. She was lucky she didn't have a roommate in her recovery room; Miriam had said she did. As it was, Leah had nobody to see her leave.

Back then, there were no electronic bracelets on wrists and ankles. There were no special alarms that went off when you crossed a certain threshold. Leah just kept her head down and walked out. She didn't know where she would go. She just knew she had to go somewhere.

Elizabeth didn't start to cry until Leah was a block away from the hospital. There was a park up ahead, another block away. Each step was painful, the whole area between Leah's legs swollen and sore. She knew she had to keep moving though.

When they got to the park, Elizabeth was crying more hysterically. Leah crouched near the bench—it was too painful to sit—then unzipped the bag and lifted the baby out. There was nobody around, so she just pulled down the front of her dress and offered the baby her breast. Elizabeth latched right on. It was as if they'd done this a million times before, as if they'd known each other for years.

As Elizabeth suckled, the reality of what Leah had done hit her. What was she going to do? She was a just-turned-sixteen-year-old with a baby, somewhere in Pasadena. She knew the hospital would report what happened, probably within the next few minutes. The police would come looking. Her parents would be notified. She could think of nothing else to do but call Miriam.

Elizabeth fed for nearly forty minutes before she slipped into a peaceful sleep. Leah held her against her chest as she walked to a pay phone on the corner. In her overnight bag, she had some loose change, some cash. Unknowingly, she had prepared for this.

When Miriam answered the phone, Leah just came out with it:

"I had my baby," she said, feeling a rush at the term—*my*

baby. "I just walked out of the hospital with her. I don't know what to do."

Miriam was quiet for a moment, and Leah feared she'd hung up. Then she said, "Where are you? I'll come get you."

Miriam showed up a half hour later, driving a red Volkswagen Beetle. She didn't even put the car in park. She just pulled up along the curb, rolled down the window, and said, "Get in."

They went to Miriam's apartment in the Valley. It was a tiny studio. The bed came down from the wall, and the kitchen was just one hot plate.

"You live here with someone?" Leah asked. She didn't see how there could possibly be room.

"Yeah, but we're rarely here at the same time. She has a boyfriend, so she's with him a lot."

Leah winced as she sat, slowly, on Miriam's couch.

"It hurts, huh?" Miriam said.

Leah just nodded. When Elizabeth whined, Leah offered her breast again.

"I don't know what I'm doing," Leah said, looking to Miriam. She felt the tears come, like a raging river heading toward a dam that was no match for it. In retrospect, it was the hormones, the exhaustion from labor, her youth. Of course she didn't know what she was doing.

"Everything will be okay," Miriam said.

Leah believed her because she needed to.

"Let's talk about the big picture, okay?" Miriam said gently.

That's when she started to ask all the tough questions that Leah had asked herself before: How are you going to provide for a baby? Where are you going to live? What about your parents?

Miriam had changed since Leah had last seen her. She was finishing high school, planning to start a job as a secretary. She had started dating a guy and had already told him she wasn't having sex until marriage. She seemed . . . *together*. Leah felt young and dumb in comparison.

"You were the one who said to keep the baby and run away," Leah said, her voice just above a whisper. She was embarrassed of how she'd clung to these words of Miriam's, words said when it was clear she wasn't thinking straight.

"I was emotional," Miriam said. "I have perspective now. I do think it was for the best, for the baby. That's what I tell myself at least."

Leah felt a heavy sadness descend as Elizabeth continued to feed. It hurt to look at her baby, at the soft hairs on her head, at the way her tiny lips moved as she suckled. Elizabeth knew nothing of the world besides Leah. Leah was her everything. And Leah was supposed to just ignore that, move on, forget.

"You will be okay," Miriam said.

Leah knew what she meant: *You will be okay when you give up your baby.* She knew then that Miriam needed Leah to make the same choice she had. Miriam needed to believe that was the right choice.

"I don't see how I could be okay," Leah said.

Tears rolled down her face, took suicidal leaps off her chin, and landed on Elizabeth's head.

"Do you want me to drive you back to the Home? To the hospital? To your parents'?" Miriam said. She presented these three options like they were the only ones.

"I can't," Leah said. "I can't just give her away and not know what happens to her. I can't."

Miriam put a hand on Leah's shoulder then used her thumb to wipe the tears from Leah's cheek.

That's when Leah got the idea, a lightbulb-over-the-head kind of idea. She looked up at Miriam.

"What if I left her with some people I know?" she said to Miriam.

Miriam looked unsure.

"I used to work at this deli. The owners, they couldn't have their own baby. They wanted one, so badly."

Leah remembered how Karen would cry any time a new mother came into the deli with a baby. She couldn't handle it. She'd ask Leah to take the order and then retreat to the back office, where Leah could hear her sniffling.

"And they're Jewish. My parents would like that," she said, still wanting to please them in some way.

"What makes you think these people would take her from you?" Miriam asked.

Miriam didn't understand. "I'd just leave her there for them. At the deli. They'll find her—like fate."

Leah didn't want to give Elizabeth to anyone, but this

scenario was better than giving her to strangers. She knew she couldn't keep her. Miriam was right about that. She was too young. She had no home, no job, no skills, no money, nobody. The Weintraubs would love Elizabeth. And, with this imagined scenario, Leah could stop by the deli occasionally, check on Elizabeth, maybe even ask to hold her. Maybe they would let her babysit. Maybe when Elizabeth was old enough, Leah could confess the truth to everyone. Maybe they would all forgive her.

Miriam agreed to drive Leah to the deli, early the next morning, around the time Leah knew Alter would show up for the day. Leah would feed Elizabeth, one last time, then leave her at the back door. Miriam and Leah would watch from across the street, make sure everything went to plan. Then they would drive away.

"Then what?" Miriam asked.

"I guess you'd take me home, to my parents," Leah said. "I'll just say I left the hospital alone, that I know nothing about what happened to the baby."

Miriam nodded, considering the plausibility of this.

"Act like you had a nervous breakdown or something," she said.

Leah didn't think it would be necessary to act.

There were so many things swept under so many rugs in those days. As Leah understood it, the hospital hadn't even reported Leah or the baby missing. They were hoping the situation would resolve itself; they didn't want this kind of thing on their record. The Home didn't want it on their record either. As far as anyone knew, Leah was safe and sound. And the baby, well, the baby's existence had been known by only a select few. As far as the other girls at the Home knew, Leah's baby had disappeared in the way all their babies were supposed to disappear—via adoption. Leah's parents, Esther at the Home, the nurses and the doctors at the hospital—none of them seemed to want to know what had really happened to the baby. Only Leah and Miriam knew that.

When "The Deli Baby" articles ran in the *Los Angeles Times*, Leah felt like just the look on her face betrayed the truth she was hiding. As she walked the halls at school, pretending to be who she'd been before Elizabeth, she felt like she was wearing a sign on her chest that said I left the baby at the deli. It was me.

She knew her parents read the paper. She knew they must have put two and two together. They didn't say anything, though. Even on their deathbeds, they never mentioned any suspicions, never asked Leah any direct questions about what had happened. They denied the existence of their grandchild to the very end.

It was in the *Los Angeles Times* articles that Leah learned the Weintraubs had changed Elizabeth's name to Deborah. Leah resented them, hated them, even though they'd had no way of knowing the name Leah had chosen. If she'd included that in the note—*Please call her Elizabeth*—they probably would have complied. The truth became obvious: Leah could only resent and hate herself.

Contrary to her initial plan, she couldn't bring herself to visit the deli, couldn't bear to see Elizabeth-Deborah. It had all been a fantasy, this idea that she would remain in her daughter's life, at a comfortable distance. It wasn't possible. It wasn't possible in the same way it wasn't possible for Leah to stay in touch with Miriam or anyone else from the Home.

Leah finished high school a year late. Her grades were awful. Her parents had all but disowned her; they gave her a roof over her head and food on her plate, reluctantly, but made it clear that she was no longer their concern once she turned eighteen. Her life became consumed by pot and Boone's Farm wine. When that got boring, she went for tequila, vodka, rum—anything that facilitated apathy. As the 1960s progressed to the seventies, there were more options for escape: cocaine, heroin, LSD. She tried everything, but she loved heroin. When she overdosed for the second time, one of her only friends, a sort-of-recovering alcoholic named Denny, dropped her off at the hospital. She was put into a state rehab program, designed to be twenty-eight days. She stayed for nearly two hundred.

Leah had kept the secret of the rape—she finally understood it for what it was—and Elizabeth for more than a decade before finally telling her therapist at the rehab program the story. Camille—that was the therapist's name.

To this day, Leah credits Camille with saving her life.

Camille warned Leah that most people leave rehab with renewed energy and are then disappointed by the same-as-it-ever-was world waiting for them. So Leah focused on creating a world that wouldn't disappoint her. She enrolled in a social work program so she could get her license to be a counselor for other women. She wanted to be someone else's Camille. She shared a condo with three other recently sober women until she saved up enough money from her part-time department store job to rent her own studio apartment. It reminded her of Miriam's studio. She wrote a letter to Miriam, apologizing for losing touch, but it was stamped return to sender. There was only the telephone book then, no internet to help with people-finding.

In the eighties, Leah started a group at the local hospital for women who had lost babies. She kept it vague—"lost babies." Most of the women who showed up had experienced miscarriages. They'd felt like failures for not being able to carry their babies to term. Leah cried when they cried—for her own failures that she was still learning to forgive.

It was one of the women in the Grief Group (as it was unofficially called) who gave Leah the idea of taking herself to a movie on Mother's Day. This particular woman didn't seek out the saddest movie she could find; she saw the outing as a way to escape the Mother's Day hullabaloo and treat herself to entertainment—a comedy or rom-com, preferably. Leah put her own masochistic twist on it by choosing the tearjerkers. After so many years of attempting to escape her pain with drugs or drink, she wanted to really feel it. She knew she had to.

She never married. Over the years, she's had only a few men in her life, always for a short time. It's been difficult to let anyone close to her. Even with all the therapy appointments she had with Camille—they saw each other regularly for nearly fifteen years before Camille retired—she hasn't been able to learn to associate sex with pleasure. She's associated it only with pain and loss and shame and guilt. She's had some attractions to women, which isn't hard to understand on a psychological level. She's never let herself go there though. Camille used to say, "You deserve to feel love." At this point though, in her seventies, Leah thinks it's too late for love—and definitely too late for sex.

It was just a few years ago that she finally found out what became of Miriam. An online search turned up her obituary. She'd died of breast cancer in 2005. Miriam had heard this was common of women who had lost children. It was like the sadness in their hearts manifested in a disease of the surrounding tissue. According to the obituary, Miriam had been married. She'd had two sons. There was, of course, no mention of the fact that she'd also had a daughter.

This year's movie, *Mothers and Daughters*, stars a roster of famous actresses—Susan Sarandon, Sharon Stone, Mira

Sorvino, Courteney Cox, Christina Ricci, Selma Blair. The story lines are mostly cheesy, melodramatic. The Selma Blair story line is particularly annoying. She finds out she's pregnant, which doesn't fit with her cool-photographer lifestyle, so she plans to have an abortion. Women in their thirties having abortions have always bothered Leah, though she knows she's supposed to be open-minded about each person's individual struggles and yada yada. She just can't figure out why someone would give up a baby when she has the means to care for the child. In any case, Selma Blair's character decides not to go through with it and then ends up falling in love with the doctor who was going to perform her abortion. Only in Hollywood.

There is one story line, though, that yanks on Leah's heartstrings. Mira Sorvino's character reveals that she gave up a baby twenty-three years ago, something she says she regrets every day, though she thinks her decision was best for her child. Her daughter tracks her down and sends her an email, inquiring about family health history. Mira Sorvino's character decides she must meet her daughter. They do, and it's a happy ending, of course. Only in Hollywood.

Leah has considered reaching out to her daughter. She's googled "Deborah Weintraub" countless times. She's seen her work profile online. She knows she's still in the Los Angeles area, working for a pharmaceutical company. She even has her phone number—or what she thinks is her phone number—written on a Post-it that she keeps folded in the zippered inner pocket of her purse.

She wonders what Deborah is like—her favorite foods, how she laughs, who she loves. Thanks to the public photos online, Leah knows Deborah looks a bit like her—the dark hair, the dark eyes a bit too close together. Deborah is middle-aged now, a fact that shocks Leah. By middle age, most people have been roughed up enough by life to be more compassionate, less judgmental toward others. Leah daydreams of Deborah forgiving her.

There have been several times that Leah has sat on her couch and started dialing the number written on the Post-it. But she's never gone through with it. What stops her is imagining Deborah chastising her: "Why call now? After all this time?" It makes her nauseated, that imagined rage.

As the credits roll and the lights come on, Leah walks out of the theater, irritated with herself for letting this silly movie get to her. She finds that sappy part of herself thinking, *Maybe I can have a Hollywood ending too.* She finds the cynical part of herself wanting a drink.

She decides to stop in the bookstore around the corner, settle her nerves with casual browsing. She selects a couple magazines from the newsstand in the front of the store, takes them to a table in the café. She notices a mother and daughter at the table next to her. She assumes they are mother and daughter; they look so alike. The mother is close to Leah's age, the daughter close to Deborah's. It's as if they have been placed there by a meddling film director looking to create a cinematic moment. Deborah starts to wonder if she's unknowingly part of a Hallmark Channel documentary.

Leah can't hear any of their conversation, but they look to be discussing something serious. She smiles to herself, imagining that this mother and daughter are meeting for the first time. She does this sometimes—imagines that her story is commonplace. She's always wanted to be ordinary.

She opens her purse, unzips the pocket that contains the Post-it note—just to see if it's still there, she tells herself. She hasn't looked at it in months. It is there, worn along the fold lines. Whenever Leah's thought of calling Deborah, she's made an event of it, spent hours on her couch at home rehearsing a speech. Maybe she needs to just do it, without all the anxiety that comes with preparation. Maybe she needs to accept the probable wrath she will incur. At least, then, she will know. At least, then, she can say she tried. At least, then, she can stop wondering.

She procrastinates by flipping through one of the magazines, mindlessly, then playing a game of Solitaire on her phone. Her heart is thumping hard and loud; she's surprised people aren't looking at her, perplexed by the sound. It's only when the mother and daughter at the table next to her get up and walk out, the daughter's arm looped through her mother's, that Leah does something she hasn't done before— she presses the last number in the sequence scribbled on the Post-it and hears a ring.

It rings once.

Twice.

Just when she's considering what to say in her voice mail, a woman answers.

"Hello?"

It occurs to Leah that this may be inappropriate—calling on Mother's Day. She hopes Deborah doesn't think she's implying that she is Deborah's mother. While she birthed her, she cannot claim that title.

Leah doesn't know what to say, but she has to say something. She's allowed too much silence after Deborah's initial greeting. She knows a dial tone is coming soon.

"Is this Deborah Weintraub?" she manages.

The woman hesitates before saying, with a professional tone, "Speaking."

Leah tries to swallow but can't.

"I don't even know where to start," Leah says, now wishing she had prepared. Her voice is shaky. "I've been wanting to call you for so long and—"

Deborah interrupts: "Was it you? At the deli?"

Her tone is not angry or bitter. She sounds only curious, fascinated even.

Leah still can't swallow. "You knew?" she says. It comes out strained.

"I found out, after my parents died. I've been wanting to find you ever since. I didn't think it would ever happen."

Leah doesn't realize tears are filling her eyes until one drops into her tea.

"I'm sorry," Leah says. "I've thought of you all the time, of course. I just . . . I didn't know if you'd want to hear from me."

"Well, at first, I didn't know if I'd want to hear from you either," she says, with a little laugh that makes Leah relax enough to sit back in her chair.

"I was only sixteen," Leah says. She's repeated these words to herself for years, like a mantra—*Iwasonlysixteen, Iwasonlysixteen, Iwasonlysixteen.*

"I know," Deborah says.

"You do?"

"Well, I assumed you were young. I never thought you didn't want me. Maybe that's my own hubris," she says. She laughs again. "I guess I just assumed you couldn't have me."

This, these words, bring such profound relief that Leah cannot speak.

"I had great parents. I've had a great life," Deborah goes on.

Leah wants to interject, to tell Deborah that she selected the Weintraubs, specifically. She didn't just leave her daughter at a random deli. *Iwasonlysixteen, Iwasonlysixteen, Iwasonlysixteen.* But this moment is not about her, about defending herself. This moment is about the two of them.

"I don't have hard feelings about it, just so you know," Deborah says. "I probably would have when I was younger. But I'm old and tired now."

They both laugh. "I'm old and tired too," Leah says. It's a dumb thing to say, but she can think of nothing else.

Deborah says, "I imagine it's been harder on you, after what you had to do."

What you had to do.

They are five minutes into knowing each other and Leah already feels understood by her daughter. In all her fantasies of this moment, she did not foresee this.

"It has been hard on me," Leah admits.

There is silence, the profound and contemplative kind. Deborah breaks it by asking, "Where do you live now?"

"I'm still in Los Angeles. You?"

Leah knows the answer but doesn't want to let on that she's tracked her daughter's whereabouts over the years. Then again, maybe Deborah would be touched to know this.

"Also in Los Angeles," she says.

There is another moment of silence before Deborah says what Leah is thinking:

"Would you want to meet? In person?"

Leah thinks of the mother-daughter duo she just witnessed, the daughter's arm looped through her mother's.

"I would love that," she says.

"Would it be ridiculous of me to suggest tomorrow?"

Leah looks around again, for the secret documentarian. She doesn't want him to miss this, her Hollywood ending.

"Tomorrow is perfect."

a good egg

MADISON IS IN the middle of a date with a less-than-interesting guy when her phone buzzes with an email notification. The guy—one of a few Mikes she's gone out with since signing up with FateFinder (the latest dating app)—is talking about his childhood on a farm in central California. He's going on and on, clearly so interested in hearing himself talk that Madison assumes he won't notice if she glances down at her phone in her lap. So that's what she does. She glances.

It's an email from YourHeritage.com. She signed up a few months ago, around the same time she signed up with the dating app. She considers all this part of her quarter-life crisis. According to YourHeritage.com, she's mostly German, with some Irish and Swedish genes mixed in there. In other words, the results confirmed that she's a boring white girl. She was hoping for a touch of American Indian, something interesting, something worth mentioning on a boring date with a boring Mike.

"There's a new connection in your family tree!"

That's what the message says. She's gotten these before. It was exciting at first, thinking she was being linked with long-lost relatives in Europe who would invite her to visit and stay in their quaint countryside cottages. But, no, most of the time the connections are fifth cousins living in Indiana or Kentucky.

The waitress comes by and asks if they want dessert. Mike looks at Madison expectantly. Everything in his smile says, "Yes! Dessert!"

"Actually, probably just the check," Madison says. The waitress leaves, and Mike looks defeated.

"Is that okay with you?" Madison asks him.

Upon realizing that she's noticed his mood change, he quickly smiles, transitioning to acting like the laid-back, "chill" guy he probably thinks women want him to be.

"Sure, sure," he says. "There's always next time."

Next time? Madison thinks. This Mike is so mistaken.

He walks her to her car—they met at the restaurant; Madison's seen too many episodes of *Dateline* to let a stranger pick her up at her apartment. When she sticks out her hand to shake his and thank him for dinner (though they split the bill, at her insistence), he bypasses the gesture and leans in to kiss her cheek. She leans away, instinctively, and he looks so hurt that she cringes.

"Sorry," she says. "I just—"

"Nah, it's okay," he says, pretending to be chill guy again.

He turns to leave, and Madison gets into her car. Her phone buzzes with another notification. This one is her mom, texting to ask how the date went. It's as if she has a tracking device on Madison. This would annoy some daughters, but Madison just considers it part of their connection. They've always had this weird psychic bond, so in tune with what each other is thinking and feeling.

Madison locks the car doors—again, too many *Dateline* episodes—and texts her mom:

"He was a dud. Going home to Frank."

Frank is her dog, a pit bull–dachshund mix that elicits stares wherever he goes. He looks like a bouncer in a club for wiener dogs.

While she's sitting there, on her phone, waiting for her mom to text back with something that makes her laugh, she checks the email from YourHeritage.com. She clicks, expecting to find another way-too-distant cousin in middle America. But this email is different. This email says they've found a "first-degree connection."

When she visits her family tree on the website, she sees they've placed this "first-degree connection" in a box just above her name, in the "mother" spot. The name is not her mother's though; the name is Dina Larkin Schmidt. This name means nothing to Madison.

Her phone buzzes with a text from her mom:

"I think you need to steer clear of the Mikes for a while."

Madison isn't even thinking about the date anymore though.

She texts her mom:

"Did you sign up for YourHeritage.com?"

She stares at the three dots on the screen, her mom in the process of crafting a response.

"No. Why? Should I?"

Madison replies:

"So weird. They just connected me to some other woman who is supposedly my mother. I should get a refund. Lol"

The dots appear again. A minute passes. The dots remain. What is her mom typing? Madison starts to wonder if this isn't a situation appropriate for a flippant "Lol." But what else could it be? She knows her mother is her mother. She's seen the photo albums. She distinctly remembers a photo of her mom in the hospital bed, cradling fresh-out-of-the-womb Madison. She was wearing a hospital gown and everything. Maybe her mother has a secret identity as Dina Larkin Schmidt. Madison saw something about this once, on *20/20* or *48 Hours*. This man had two separate families, living just an hour apart, and they had no idea each other existed.

"Can Dad and I come by?"

That's all her mom's message says. Three minutes of dots on the screen, and that's all she says.

Madison's palms get clammy.

"I'll come there. I'm close."

When Madison arrives, her parents are waiting on the front porch, sitting on the bench that nobody ever uses. They look like a cover of *Sunset* magazine. When Madison approaches, they stand, each wearing strange smiles that Madison hasn't seen before.

"Hey, sweetie," her mom says. She is quite obviously nervous, shaken even.

"You guys are being weird. What's wrong?"

"Nothing is *wrong*," her dad says, but just the emphasis on the word *wrong* tells her that something is, by most people's definitions, not *right*.

"Sit," her mom says.

They all sit on the bench, which is awkward because it's more of a love seat for two people. Madison is between them, feeling suddenly like she's five years old.

"Just tell me what's going on," she says.

"So, this is going to blow your mind," her dad says, with a strange chuckle.

"When we were in our thirties, trying to have a baby, we weren't having much luck," her mom says.

Madison tucks her hands under her thighs, braces herself for the news that she's adopted, that the hospital photos she's remembering were all staged, part of a charade. She looks like her parents though. People say things like "spitting image" when they see her with her dad.

"We thought about adopting, but I really wanted to carry a child of my own. I wanted that experience," her mom says.

Now Madison is thoroughly confused.

"The doctors presented us with some options," her dad says.

It's like they've rehearsed this, practiced whose lines are whose.

"And we decided to use a donor egg," her mom says.

They both look at her, awaiting her reaction. At first, Madison has no reaction. What she pictures is a chicken egg being transferred from one set of hands to another—a gifted egg, a donated egg. She thinks of Easter, which is coming up; she'd told her mom she'd make a fruit salad.

"A donor egg?" she says.

They both nod. "A young woman donated her eggs to us, and they joined them with your dad's sperm and—"

Madison puts her hands up, like *Stop!* She does not want to hear anything about her father's sperm.

"I get it," she says.

She actually knows of a friend of a friend who donated her eggs. She made thousands of dollars, apparently, and used it to buy Oxycontin. Then she dropped out of college.

"It's not as uncommon as you might think," her mom says. She must notice the confusion on Madison's face. "I mean, there are all these celebrities getting pregnant at fifty. That's not really *possible*, you know?"

Madison doesn't know, not really. Though, she does remember being surprised by the news that Janet Jackson was pregnant.

"Did you, like, *know* her?" Madison asks. "The egg donor woman?"

Her mom nods, vigorously. "Honey, we received all kinds of information about her. We wouldn't have made this decision if we didn't have as many facts as possible."

"But you didn't get her name?" Madison asks.

Her mom and dad look at each other and then at their daughter-from-another-woman's-egg.

"I'm guessing it's Diana, the woman you found online."

"Dina," Madison says, feeling irrationally annoyed with her mom's failure to get the name right. "And I didn't *find* her."

"Dina. Right. Dina," her mom says.

"There were no online family trees back when we did this," her dad says. "There was no online *anything* when we did this."

"We couldn't have known you would find out this way," her mom adds.

Madison gets up from the bench, feeling suddenly claustrophobic and hot. She faces her parents, hands on her hips.

"Were you just never going to tell me?" she asks.

They both shrug—synchronized shrugging.

"We didn't think it was that important," her dad says.

"I carried you for nine months, I delivered you. We raised you. We just didn't think it . . . mattered," her mom says, biting her lip.

"It kind of matters that some other woman is my biological mother," Madison says, though she's not quite sure why this matters. It's just odd that there is a woman out in the world, a woman named Dina Larkin Schmidt, who probably looks like her. Maybe this woman is the reason Madison's needed glasses since she was a kid. Maybe this woman is the reason Madison wants to be a doctor. Her parents are artist types— her mom teaches painting classes, her dad builds cabinets— and they have 20/20 vision.

"What if there are others out there, from her eggs?" Madison says, her mind racing with the possibilities. She could be interacting with half-siblings on a daily basis and not know it. One of the Mikes could be her half-sibling. She shudders. She might need to update her dating profile with this information: I'm born of an unknown egg donor—beware.

"There aren't," her mom says. "We paid an extra amount to ensure this donor would donate only one time, to us. We are the legal owners of all the eggs they retrieved from her."

"*All* her eggs? Like, how many?"

"There were around twenty, if I remember correctly," her mom says.

"You were the embryo that stuck," her dad says. He looks proud.

"What happened to the other eggs?"

"They stayed in a freezer, in case we wanted to give you a sibling. We decided we were so lucky to have you, and you were more than enough," her mom says.

"And then?"

"They were disposed of," her dad says. "According to the contract."

"The contract," Madison says. "Right."

Nobody says anything for a good minute or two.

Then her dad says, "Do you want to contact this woman?"

"Dina," her mom says, placing a hand on his arm, reminding him that she is not just "this woman."

"Maybe," Madison says. "I don't know."

Her parents seem terribly nervous. Madison feels bad for them, in a way. It's like they think she's going to stop coming to Christmas dinner at their house and start opening presents under the tree with Dina Larkin Schmidt.

"I'm just curious," Madison says. "I'm allowed to be curious, right?"

"Of course," they say in unison.

Her dad stands and gives her a hug. "We trust you," he says, "to do whatever you think is right."

Her mom remains seated, still wearing her nervous smile.

When Madison gets back to her apartment, her new roommate, Alyssa, is watching a recording of *The Bachelor* and eating popcorn. Frank is in Alyssa's lap. He barely knows her; he just wants access to the popcorn. Alyssa makes small talk, asks about Madison's day. Madison's never liked this about having roommates—the lack of quiet. As an only child, she's accustomed to quiet.

She doesn't tell Alyssa anything about Dina Larkin Schmidt. She doesn't know what there is to tell yet; the story is incomplete. She escapes to her room, Frank at her heels, and opens her laptop. It occurs to her that Dina must have received the same "first-degree connection" message from YourHeritage.com. Maybe she'll be the first to email. Madison's in-box is empty though, so she takes to Google.

The internet doesn't offer much about Dina Larkin Schmidt. It appears she's a nurse at Cedars-Sinai, so she's in Los Angeles. Some additional sleuthing reveals she's a Labor and Delivery nurse—slightly ironic. She has a Facebook page, but it's private. The small profile picture is of Dina with a man—probably her husband. They are both wearing sunglasses. The only thing Madison can analyze is the smile. She supposes Dina's is similar to her own. When Dina smiles, her lips disappear completely; Madison has this same affliction.

She decides she'll wait a few days, see if Dina contacts her first. If she doesn't, maybe that means she has no interest in knowing Madison. And then Madison will have to decide if she has interest in knowing her.

On day three, Madison receives an email, not from Dina, but from someone with her last name—Garrett Schmidt. The subject line just says: Looking for Information. Madison thinks, *Yeah, me too*, and taps her phone to open the message.

> Dear Madison,
>
> Hi. My name is Garrett Schmidt. I submitted my
> wife's DNA to YourHeritage.com for her birthday and
> just received a strange message connecting you as
> her daughter. I'm guessing this is a mistake. I've sent
> an email to customer service. But I figured I'd reach
> out to you anyway. Sorry for this strange message.
>
> —Garrett

Madison isn't sure what she should say, or if she should
say anything at all. It's clear Garrett doesn't know about
Dina's egg-donating past. Or, if he does, he doesn't realize
that one of the eggs became a human. Men are dumb about
anything related to female anatomy.

Would it affect their marriage if Garrett found out about
his wife's biological daughter? Do they have kids of their
own? Would those kids want to meet Madison, their half-
sibling? It's all too much to consider. Madison types and
deletes several different responses then settles on being
honest, straightforward.

> Dear Garrett,
>
> Hello. Yes, quite a weird situation. Apparently,
> Dina donated her eggs years ago . . . to my parents.

One of those eggs became me. A good egg, if I do say so myself. Anyway, it's likely Dina never considered this would happen. I don't really know what else to say. I'm open to meeting, if you want. Sorry for my equally strange message.

—Madison

She hits send and then waits, expecting an immediate reply. Her message is deserving of an immediate reply, after all. But, when a couple hours pass and she's tired of pacing, she realizes that Garrett does not think so.

It's two days later when he finally responds.

Hi, Madison. Apologies for the delay. This has been a lot to take in. Dina and I just adopted a child, actually. A boy, from Guatemala. It's been two years in the making. So, we've been busy.

I hope this does not come across wrong, but I think it would be best if I didn't mention this to Dina right now. She's been emotional as it is, with the new addition. We were not able to have children of our own, so she might have complicated feelings about this situation. Maybe a meeting can be arranged at a later date. I hope you understand, and I appreciate your discretion.

Her *discretion*? She's surprised by the insta-nausea. She

didn't think this man, this stranger, could have such an effect on her. She didn't think she cared that much about meeting Dina. But now that she's been rejected—that's what it feels like, at least—she knows she did care. She knows she does care, still.

She doesn't respond. She hates Garrett Schmidt now, thinks he should go by Garrett Schmuck. She feels sorry for her biological mother, being married to someone who says "at a later date." Even if he is cringeworthy, it is sad, though, about their not being able to have a child of their own. Ironic too. Maybe Dina gave all her could-have-been-babies to Madison's parents, unknowingly. Maybe women are granted only so many, the grand sum always a mystery.

Madison decides she wants to see Dina, just *see* her. In person. She won't say anything—because Garrett Schmuck appreciates her *discretion*. She just wants to watch her go about her daily life. Is she a nice person? Does she say "excuse me" when she accidentally bumps someone's elbow? Does she have a long torso like Madison? Does she laugh easily? Can she parallel park? These things feel important to know.

All Madison knows is her place of employment, so she decides to go there. She calls first, posing as a patient wanting to deliver thank-you flowers to Nurse Schmidt. "She'll be here Saturday," the woman on the phone says. This woman has obviously not seen enough *Dateline* episodes.

When she shows up at the Labor and Delivery unit, she doesn't have a specific plan in mind. She decides she'll just . . . linger. She figures she looks like a loved one, awaiting the arrival of a new niece or nephew or cousin or sibling or whatever. The unit is chaotic, so her presence isn't that noticeable. There are two women walking the halls, in active labor, their husbands trailing after them looking helpless and scared.

Madison takes a seat in the waiting room. About-to-be grandparents sit in the chairs on one side of her; just-became grandparents sit in the chairs on the other side. Balloons and bouquets and running doctors pass through the hallway. Everyone is on a phone.

There are more nurses milling about than she expected. Every time a new one passes by, she stares at the name tag. Most of them don't notice the staring, but a couple do and seem unnerved. She's about twenty minutes into her spy mission when she sees a new face at the nurses' station. She sits up taller in her chair, trying to get a better look. The woman has the same basic features as the woman in the Facebook profile picture—brown hair, in her late thirties or early forties. She is chatting with another nurse, a younger nurse. They laugh about something then give each other a little fist bump. Madison's biological mother is a woman who fist-bumps.

Dina—Madison is now certain this is Dina—leaves the nurses' station, walking toward Madison. Madison holds the armrest of her chair, squeezing tightly, reminding herself of how her mom used to grip the door handle when teaching her to drive. "That isn't going to help if I crash," Madison had told her at the time. She was such a brat when she was a teenager. And, yet, her mom still loved her, all the while knowing she shared none of her genes.

Madison exhales when Dina passes by. She's going to the elevators. Madison turns, watches her push the down button. It must be her break time. Madison decides to follow. There are a couple other people waiting for the elevator; Dina won't even notice her.

It's strange, standing right behind her in the elevator, close enough to see the small hairs on the back of her neck, the ones that refuse to be swept up into her ponytail. They are about the same height, the same build—small-boned, thin. Madison's mom has that build too. She imagines her mom perusing egg donors, selecting one who shared some of her own physical characteristics—probably not because she wanted to fool Madison, but because she wanted to fool herself.

When they exit the elevator, Dina heads for the courtyard, Madison a safe distance behind her. In the courtyard, a man and a boy are waiting at a picnic table, a cooler with them. It takes Madison just a few seconds to realize that this must be Garrett Schmuck and the Guatemalan adopted son. Madison stops abruptly, sits on a bench, her view (and their view of her) partially obscured by a tree.

The boy doesn't see Dina at first. He is facing Garrett, his new father. He must be about four or five years old, old enough to know he was taken from one life and put into another. He is wearing an Old Navy T-shirt and jeans with Adidas sneakers. He has already been transformed into an American.

Dina crouches down and says, "Seb?"

Seb—probably short for Sebastian. Madison wonders if it's the name he was born with, the one he's known for his years on Earth so far. She hopes so. It sounds like it is; she can picture the accent mark over the "a"—Sebastián. It would be nice of them not to change it, nice of them to consider his feelings instead of naming him something trendy like Asher or Finn or Silas.

Seb turns around, and his face changes completely when he sees Dina. His smile, so big, pushes his cheeks so far upward that his eyes become little slits. He runs toward Dina. Her arms are out to him, and he falls right into them. It's like they haven't seen each other in weeks, like this is a scene at an airport.

Dina kisses his cheeks and musses his hair. Garrett looks on, seeming less Schmuck-like and more Aw-shucks-like. He puts the cooler on the table and starts to unpack it, revealing plastic-wrapped sandwiches, a paper plate with cheese and crackers, some strawberries, cupcakes. Madison makes a mental note to add "picnics" to her list of interests on her dating profile.

It makes sense now, why Garrett didn't want Madison to meet Dina. Not right now, at least. She seems so happy with Seb, but it's a new happiness, fragile in its infancy. Madison decides she'll set a notification in her phone, a reminder to get in touch with Garrett every six months. She will ask, "Is now a better time?" And, some day, he will say, "Yes."

As Seb goes straight for a cupcake, Madison gets teary-eyed, caught up in this moment that doesn't belong to her. Then her phone buzzes and the moment ends.

It's a text, from her mom:

Was just thinking of you.

Of course she was. Her timing is, once again, impeccable.

Madison replies:

Sushi tonight? My treat.

Her mom:

Sure! What did I do to deserve this?

Madison thinks for a second and then responds:

Everything.

the narrative of us

SHE HAS BEEN sleeping since ten. It's noon now. A two-hour nap is unheard of. We are usually grateful for forty-five minutes, enough time to feed ourselves and tend to basic hygiene. Twenty minutes is the norm. The books say newborns sleep all the time. I've started to hate the books. "She doesn't really nap," we'd told the doctor. He didn't give us much advice. He was in a hurry to tend to his other patients. "We're knee-deep in flu season," he'd said.

I listen for the telltale whimper that will become a cry if we do not go in to rescue her. All I hear is the static of the white noise machine. The books say it mimics the sounds of the womb—the whoosh of blood rushing through arteries, the gurgling of digestion, the echoing beat of the heart. In these first few months, we are supposed to ease her transition from my belly to the world with this white noise. We are supposed to swaddle her in blankets so she can't move her limbs. We are supposed to rock her and bounce her because she spent all those months being jostled around inside me while I went about my daily routines. This is all she knows.

Jake is quiet, on his laptop, standing at the kitchen island. He never sits now. "You're like a horse," I told him the other day as he ate pizza while standing, refusing to join me for a rare moment of quiet on the couch.

"Working?" I ask him.

I'm taking six months off from my job at the library, mostly unpaid, because that's how this country operates. Jake's company allowed him to cobble together paternity leave time with unused vacation hours to take a month off. When he went back, he got approval to work from home a couple days a week. It's nice having him, even if he's usually busy taking calls or pecking away at his computer. He never learned to type properly, something I tease him about whenever an opportunity presents itself. Now, though, I am not in the mood for teasing.

"Yeah," he says, not looking up. "I've got this big forecast report due."

Do you think she's okay in there? I want to ask him this question, but I refrain. I know he's tired of this particular question. I asked it so often while I was pregnant: *Do you think she's okay in there?* We held our collective breath all those months, closing our eyes at the start of each ultrasound scan, hoping our little girl would go on living, unlike her brother before her. Now that she is here, I am supposed to be done with all my fretting. Instead, I've had this startling realization that she was much safer in my womb, despite its less-than-reliable history. Out here, in the world, there are so many new dangers.

When she emerged—twenty-three hours after I felt my first contraction while we watched the first game of the World Series—she was purple and silent, not pink and screaming like all the babies born on sitcoms.

"Is she okay?" I asked the scrubs-clad nurses surrounding us. I repeated this question more times than I can remember.

"We need her to scream," one of them said.

"What's her name, hon?" asked Nurse Wendy, the nurse who had held one of my legs—Jake held the other—during the pushing. Just a couple days ago, I got around to writing thank-you notes and sent one to Wendy. *I know you help women give birth all the time, and you might not even remember me, but I am so grateful for you.*

"Mia," I said, my eyes fixed on our purple, silent baby as she was transferred from one blue-gloved person to another.

We chose "Mia" from a list of Italian baby names on a website. We wanted a name that would go well with Jake's very-Italian last name (Mancini). Mia means "mine" or "wished-for child."

"Okay, Mia. Give us a scream, sweetheart," Nurse Wendy said.

And, as if Mia was listening and understood the directive, she screamed, her face turning slowly from purple to pink.

They lay her on my chest, the gray umbilical cord still connecting us. They gave Jake the scissors to cut the cord. It wasn't the soft, pliable thing I'd imagined. It was stiff as a garden hose. I watched the muscles of his hands contract as he separated Mia and me. Sadness passed over me in that moment. We would never be physically connected again. Just like that, she was on her own.

The chair reserved for exhausted spouses did not look comfortable, so I told Jake to go home and rest. He did not protest. Nurses came and went throughout the night and into the early morning, taking various vital signs. I stared at Mia in her plastic bassinet next to my bed, all six pounds of her wrapped in the pink-and-blue-striped hospital blanket. She looked so small, like a fragile porcelain doll. I didn't even try to sleep.

Just after dawn, the pediatrician came to see us. He was a petite Asian man, gentle-seeming. He changed Mia's diaper and listened to her heart and bent and straightened her legs a few times.

"Be sure to keep her home for the first eight weeks," he said, giving me a smile that did not match the sternness of his tone.

"Eight weeks? Really?"

"Yes, it's just not worth the risk."

I must have looked perplexed, in a fog of hormone-induced bliss, because he went on to explain that a local mother had taken her newborn to a wedding recently, where someone with herpes had kissed the baby, transmitting the virus.

"The baby's immune system was too immature to fight it," he said.

I must have still looked perplexed, because he then informed me that the baby had died.

"So, keep her at home," he said, with another incongruent smile.

Then he left.

I googled the story, hoping it was a fable he'd created for the purposes of instilling fear in new mothers anxious to introduce their babies to swarms of family and friends. But no—it was true. The baby was named Liliana. There was a picture of her, wrapped in a blanket similar to Mia's, in the arms of her father, a hospital band still on his wrist. There was another picture of her hooked up to various tubes and machines, her tiny mouth open, naked except for a diaper. Why did the family allow these pictures to be published? When I started crying, Mia looked at me like *What's the matter?* I was still crying when Jake arrived at the hospital, bags under his eyes. I told him about Liliana. I told him what the doctor had said.

"What an asshole" was his response.

Jake has told me I need to put down the phone. I'm always on it, googling while Mia is latched onto my breast. I want to know what green poop means, how to tell if Mia is eating enough, if the flaky skin on her scalp is harmless cradle cap or eczema. The internet says that babies with eczema may be prone to food allergies, which leads me down a rabbit hole of research into anaphylactic shock. I get lost in these dark, deep rabbit holes, looking at photos of horrible diaper rash, perusing statistics about sudden infant death syndrome.

I made Jake move all the medications and cleaning supplies to upper cabinets, even though it will be months before Mia can crawl, even though she can't grab her feet yet, even though she doesn't realize she *has* feet yet. I've already started worrying about the toilets. I've read that babies can drown in them. I've ordered various kinds of safety latches from Amazon.

When our neighbor, Gwen, a retired kindergarten teacher, stops to peer into the stroller when I take Mia for a walk, I feel a rush of adrenaline as she comments on how adorable Mia is. *You can't have her*, I think. I ask Jake to stick a piece of wood in the track of the window in Mia's room, so it can't be easily slid open by an intruder. I don't tell Jake that it's Gwen I fear. Gwen, with her arthritic knees. Gwen, who brings us a basket of oranges from her tree once a month.

I don't tell Jake about any of my racing thoughts, my fears. I don't tell him that when Mia's quiet in the car, sitting in her seat facing away from me, I think she has somehow suffocated herself on the blanket I use to cover her legs. I don't tell him that when I return from a trip to the grocery store after leaving Mia at home with him, I expect to see ambulances outside, lights flashing, neighbors standing around, looks of pity on their faces as they all wonder how they're going to tell me the unthinkable has happened. I don't tell him that I can hear the sound of Mia's skull cracking against the stone tile floor when I imagine tripping and falling while holding her. I don't tell him that I can see her facedown on the floor, unconscious, after rolling off the bed because I turned away for that one second I'll regret the rest of my life. I don't tell him that I can hear her struggle to breathe as something—a quarter, a key, a grape—gets stuck in her throat. I don't tell him that I can see her at the bottom of the pool, as purple as she was the day she emerged from me.

I don't tell him these things because I know they will confirm the suspicions he harbored during the days after we lost Ben, suspicions that I've lost it, that I am a person capable of losing it.

It is now 12:15 p.m. I tap the Instagram icon on my phone. I enter the name of a former coworker, the woman whose son died in his sleep. I remember the day we found out. I had just started the job, an entry-level position at a marketing firm (a position so unbearable that I decided to go back to school for a degree in library science). There was a company-wide email, audible gasps. Everyone chipped in money to help pay the funeral expenses. I think I gave twenty dollars. This was before I met Jake, before I even thought of becoming a mother. I would give a thousand dollars now, with the childish hope that doing so would earn me the good karma necessary to avoid a similarly tragic fate.

Sharon is her name, the coworker. She has thousands of followers on Instagram, likely voyeurs looking for her to show them that it's possible to go on when the worst happens. Sharon's smiling in her photos. I wonder if the smiles are genuine. I wonder how they could be. I heard someone say once that when you lose a child, you spend the rest of your life impersonating who you used to be. That sounds about right. She has three children now, including one who was born after the boy died. *At least she has them*, I think. Which is probably an awful thing to think. It's not as if the presence of these three negates the absence of the one.

Jake and I will have only Mia. I tell people this and they say, "Oh, you'll forget how hard these early days are and you'll have another one." They don't know that I made Jake get a vasectomy right after Mia was born because I couldn't bear the thought of losing another baby. They don't know that I feel so lucky—so astonishingly lucky—to have Mia, that I have no interest in pressing that luck. You know, I thought having Mia would heal me from losing Ben, but that's not the case at all. The pain is worse, in a way, because Mia is evidence of who Ben could have been.

"She's been sleeping a long time now," I say. I cannot help myself.

Jake looks up. He registers the near-panic I am trying to conceal.

"Do you want me to go check on her?" he says.

There is concern in his tone, concern he won't admit to. I am the worrier of the two of us. That is our narrative— me, dramatic fretter; Jake, the rational stoic. When we were dating, analyzing every inch of each other, I noticed this strange line pattern on Jake's palm. The top line, the one that usually curves upward toward the fingers, went straight across until it ran right into the line below. I was fascinated by this, by everything about Jake then. I looked it up online. "It's called a simian line," I marveled. According to the internet, his head line "captures" his heart line. This means he operates with nearly all logic, little emotion. Apparently, Hillary Clinton and Tony Robbins have the same kind of simian line. Mia has it too. I hope this means she will be spared some of the emotional angst I suffered from adolescence through my early twenties. I hope this means she won't inherit my insomnia-causing worrying.

Jake worries too, though. I know this. I keep this secret for him.

A week ago, I was awakened in the middle of the night— not by the baby, but by rustling from our bedroom, which is no longer "ours" since Jake's been sleeping there alone while I sleep on a mattress in Mia's room. This was a plan I made when pregnant, thinking I would be one of the cool wives who let her husband rest while she managed the night feedings. "I have the boobs. It just makes sense," I'd told Jake. I imagined Jake telling his friends this. I imagined their envy, their "I wish Amanda/Erin/Renee was like that." I imagined Jake's pride. Now though, with the baby here, I understand why my friends-with-children scoffed at my plans: "You're going to want him to help," one said. "Misery loves company."

I wasn't sure if I should take the baby with me to investigate the rustling or leave her in the bassinet. What if a burglar was ransacking the house? I decided to leave her and tiptoed into the hallway, calling Jake's name in a tentative whisper. There was no response.

When I peeked into the room, Jake was standing next to the bed, throwing off all the pillows and the comforter in a frantic frenzy.

"Jake?" I said.

He didn't look at me though. He rummaged around in the sheets, eventually pulling them off, revealing the bare mattress beneath.

"Jake?" I said. "What are you doing?"

He looked at me, startled. His eyes were wide open, but he didn't seem to be *there*. I knew then that he was sleepwalking. My sister was a sleepwalker. The family loves to tell the story of how I walked in on her once with her hand in the bird's cage, petting our parakeet while humming the theme song to *Full House*.

"I can't find her," Jake said. He was tossing around the sheets, looking under the comforter in a heap on the floor.

"Who?" I asked.

"The baby. I can't find the baby," he said. "She was right here."

I went to him then, trying to remember what they say about waking a sleepwalker. Was it a good thing or a bad thing? I couldn't remember, but I had to touch him, to tell him that Mia was fine.

"The baby's with me," I said. "In her room."

He looked at me like I'd gone mad. Up close, I could see his face was red and sweaty with his panicked efforts.

"She was right here."

I shook my head. "No, she wasn't. She's been with me. Do you want to see?"

He woke up then. And when he did, he was disoriented, unsure what we were doing standing there, the room a mess.

"I'm so tired," he said. That was it. He fell onto the bare mattress and went to sleep, snoring within five minutes.

The next day, he asked me why the sheets were on the floor. I told him he'd had a nightmare. That's what losing a baby is—the worst of nightmares.

"I'll go check on her," Jake says. "Just let me finish this email."

He resumes his typing—his pecking—and I wonder if this is it, the moment we'll remember as the dividing line between "before Mia died" and "after Mia died."

I imagine Jake going to her room, me on his heels, the

familiar creak of the door pulling away from the jamb, the white noise machine blaring. I imagine him going to her bassinet, peering inside: "Mia? Mia?" I imagine him shaking her, saying, "Fuck." I imagine going to him and saying, "What? What is it?" I am dizzy because I know. I imagine reaching for her. She is cold, and I shriek. It is a sound I've never made before and, confused, I look around for who has made this horrific sound. I imagine him telling me to call 9-1-1 while he tries the chest compressions we learned in that baby safety class, the class with the videos from 1980s that we made fun of, the class we spent playing tic-tac-toe on the back of a brochure about babyproofing.

I imagine how the memories of her will simultaneously comfort and torment me. The way she giggled when we held her high above our heads and flew her around the room, shouting, "Super Mia!" The way she'd fall asleep in her swing with her hands in midair—"zombie hands" we called them. The way Jake would muss up her hair—she was born with so much of it—and make her look like a Troll doll. The way she cooed at the ceiling fan, our makeshift mobile. The way she smiled at the dogs with increasing charm, like she was trying so hard to get a smile in response. She has Jake's eyes, the smiling eyes, little crescent moons of joy. They are his father's eyes. I think of him often. And Jake's mom too. Just like Mia's presence makes me sad all over again about the son we could have had, it also makes me sad about the grandparents she should have had. They would have adored her. She is easy to adore.

Jake closes his laptop, and I follow him to Mia's room, holding a breath tightly in my chest. He opens the door. He turns off the white noise. I close my eyes. It is silent. And then it is not. Mia babbles, stringing together various vowel sounds in her usual greeting.

"Hello, my girl. Did you have a big sleep?" Jake says to her.

Mia wriggles with excitement in her swaddling blanket, her fists punching against the muslin fabric, eager to be free, to reach out toward us, her parents, her people, her everything in this world. Her cheeks are rosy, her hair slick with sweat. She smiles her still-toothless grin, and those little crescent moons appear. Sometimes, in those moons, I can see her as a five-year-old running in the waves at the beach. Sometimes, in those moons, I can see her on her wedding day, Jake walking her down the aisle. Sometimes, in those moons, I can see her holding her own baby.

I kneel next to the bassinet, nuzzle into her neck, blow raspberries that make her squirm and giggle. She is sticky and warm and sweet-smelling and alive. Jake lifts her out, frees her from the swaddle. She stretches as he places her on the changing table.

"She's okay," I whisper to Jake, mesmerized, relieved.

"Of course she is," he says, like I'm crazy, in accordance with the narrative of us.

Yes, I think. *Of course she is.*

acknowledgments

This book is incredibly personal to me, so the first person I want to thank is YOU. Yes, you. I really appreciate you going on this little book journey and getting to know these characters.

My husband, Chris, and I had four pregnancy losses before welcoming our daughter. In the months after her birth, I did not have the energy or focus to work on a conventional novel. Instead, I started working on stories about motherhood. Over time, I realized all the stories were connected, which makes sense—since becoming a mother, I've never felt more connected to other women and to human beings in general. Life is so fragile and hard and beautiful. We are all stumbling through it together. Sometimes our paths are parallel, sometimes they cross.

Thank you to Jessica Berger Gross, the editor of *About What Was Lost: Twenty Writers on Miscarriage, Healing, and Hope*. This book was a true comfort during my pregnancy losses. It contains an essay by Rebecca Johnson ("Risky

Business"), which gave me the title for this book. The line in her essay is: "As a fertility doctor whom I interviewed once said to me, 'Nature is extraordinarily wasteful when it comes to reproduction—look at all the acorns on the forest floor.'" Thank you, Rebecca.

Thank you to Ann Fessler and her book *The Girls Who Went Away: The Hidden History of Women Who Surrendered Children for Adoption in the Decades Before Roe v. Wade.* So many of the voices in this book influenced Leah's story.

Thank you to all the women who have shared stories of motherhood (the losses and the gains) via blog posts, essays, articles, message boards, emails and text messages. There are too many to name. So many of your words helped shape the characters in this book. Your vulnerability and honesty are an inspiration.

Thank you to Shel for showing me how tenacious love can be. Watching you with "your Chris" has made me a better partner to "my Chris."

Thank you to Nick, Sara, Kaity, and Michael for giving your blessing to this book.

Thank you to Meredith for reading a first draft, and to my mom, who reads every first draft.

Thank you to the dream team at Turner and Keylight— Todd Bottorff, Stephanie Beard, Heather Howell, Kathleen Timberlake, and everyone behind the scenes. You do publishing how publishing should be done. Thank you to Lauren Peters-Collaer for the beautiful cover—I made it into a poster in my office. And thank you to Carey Nelson Burch—I am so happy to have you as my wing woman.

Chris, I always save you and our girl for last, that spot that is typically reserved for "the best." We have been through so much together and it hasn't always been easy or pretty. But look at us. This life we have made together, this daughter we have together—just thinking about my gratitude makes me teary eyed (and we both know I'm not much of a crier). Thank you for letting me be me. It is the greatest gift you could give. I love you.

And, to Mya: This book wouldn't exist if you didn't. It's that simple. You have opened my heart in ways I never thought possible. I promise to be the best mom I can be for you, even (or especially) when you insist on reading twelve books at bedtime. And if you proclaim hatred of all books in your teenage years, that's cool too. Just be you, with grit and without apology. I love you.

NO HIDING IN BOISE by KIM HOOPER

COMING SUMMER 2021

ANGIE

My ring tone is the theme song from "Sesame Street." We just started letting Evie watch "Sesame Street" even though the American Academy of Pediatrics has strict rules about screen time for children under the age of 2 (Evie will be 2 in a few months). The American Academy of Pediatrics must not understand the daily lives of families, the need for distraction during chaotic mornings. The only way I can get ready for work is by putting Evie in her high-chair and letting her watch Elmo while eating oatmeal by the fistfuls. Cale hates the oatmeal because she gets it all over herself. He suggests I buy toaster waffles and I suggest he make breakfast—it's the same boring dance we do. Anyway, Evie loves the oatmeal, and it's healthy. The American Academy of Pediatrics would approve.

Last week, while assembling dinner—I do not cook, I assemble pre-made items from the refrigerated section of Trader Joe's—I'd started humming the "Letter of the Day" song that Elmo sings in every episode. Cale laughed. He was in one of his rare chipper moods and I thought, "Maybe this will work out after all." "This" being our marriage, our existence together as parents. When I went to the bathroom, he set the "Sesame Street" theme song as my ringtone. He probably assumed I'd change it back, but I kept it, as a reminder that he still has good days.

The phone rings in the middle of a recurring dream in which I cannot remember the combination to my high school locker. By the time I realize the ringing is not part of the dream, by the time I reach over to the nightstand, fumbling around for the phone, the ringing has stopped. The missed call is a number I don't recognize. It's just after midnight, a cruel time for a robocall. Must be a wrong number. I close my eyes, tell myself to go back to sleep, but then it rings again.

I answer this time, so I can curse at the caller. There's something empowering about cursing at a stranger. I know I shouldn't think this, but life has been stressful and releasing a good "fuck you" takes the edge off.

"Who is this?" I whisper, not wanting to wake Cale. He's been taking something called Trazodone at night lately, for sleep. This means I'm the one who has to be ready to tend to Evie if she cries. It's a role I resent because I've had it since she was born. She's been sleeping through the night for a while now, but she still has bad nights—usually due to teething or pee somehow escaping her diaper and soaking her pajamas.

"Is this Ms. Matthews?"

It's a man. He sounds stern. This is not a robocall or a wrong number.

"Yes," I whisper, now more concerned than angry.

"Ma'am, this is Officer Stokes with the Boise Police Department," he says.

My first thought is Evie, though I know she's just down the hall, in her crib. I can hear the white noise machine whirring over the monitor.

"I'm sorry to disturb you at this hour, but we think your husband was involved in a shooting at Ray's Bar. He's been transferred to St. Al's."

I'm quite confident this man has his facts wrong. Cale isn't at a bar; he's in bed next to me.

I turn in bed to wake Cale so he can tell this officer himself that there has been a misunderstanding.

But, he's not there.

"Ma'am?" the man on the phone says.

I get out of bed, walk to the bathroom, sure I'll find Cale there, sitting on the toilet looking at me like I'm a mad woman. He's not there though.

"Just a minute," I tell the officer.

I walk upstairs, hoping Cale is getting a midnight snack, though I've never seen him do such a thing. Cale doesn't believe in snacking, takes joy in fasting as long as he can and then eating an entire pizza.

"Ma'am?" the officer says again.

I can hear sirens in the background.

"I...I don't understand," I tell him.

"You can call the hospital for updates," he says. The sirens are louder.

"You said you think it's him? So, you're not sure?"

This woman at work, a fellow copywriter, told me that phrase—grasping at straws—is from a proverb about a drowning man reaching desperately at the surrounding grasses as he goes under. This is what I feel like right now—like I'm drowning.

"We retrieved his ID and your contact information from his wallet," he says.

The contact information. I know what he means. When I moved in with Cale and realized how often he went biking in the foothills alone, I insisted he carry certain things with him—his ID, his phone, his health insurance card, and my contact information. I'd written my name and number on a notecard, under the words, "In case of emergency" and folded it in half. He rolled his eyes at me, but he complied. I'd watched him slip it into his wallet.

"I'm sorry to give you this news," the officer says.

He ends the call before I can think to ask the obvious questions:

What happened?

Was he shot?

Is he going to be okay?

I know I should be focused on that, on Cale being okay, but I can't help but fixate on another question: What was he doing at Ray's bar in the middle of the night? I know that place, I've driven by it. It's a dive, on a quiet side street on the outskirts of downtown. From the street, there's just a brick wall, a single black door, and a sign above it that says RAY'S.

If Cale wanted a beer at midnight (which would be strange), why not get one from our kitchen? We always have a few half-full six-packs in the fridge. Or, if he had to go to a bar (which would be even stranger), why not just walk five minutes up 13th Street? Why get in the car and drive across town?

Plain and simple, it doesn't make sense that he was doing anything at midnight, let alone sitting at a bar. Since we've had Evie, we go to bed by eight. Both of us are exhausted. When I put her to sleep at seven, my shoulders relax away from my ears just slightly and I take pleasure in a glass of wine and whatever I've assembled for dinner. We barely make it through one episode of a show everyone says we "have to watch"—"Stranger Things" being the latest—then claim fatigue in a defeatist way and trudge to our bedroom. Cale's been having trouble with waking up in the middle of the night and not being able to fall asleep again—hence, the pills. I've known about that. I've known he's been "off." But I never would have guessed he'd be going to a bar at midnight.

I try to call him, hoping he'll defy what the police officer told me and pick up his phone. It goes straight to voicemail though, Cale's voice deep and strong, telling me to leave a message. I do, because it means I'm doing something:

"It's me. I hope you're okay. Please call me. I love you."

We haven't said those three words to each other in a while—I love you. We've said, "love you" in a slapdash way when saying goodbye in the morning. We let the words run together, thoughtlessly—"loveyou." Our sex life is just as slapdash—a once-every-few-weeks item on a mental checklist. I haven't been trying hard enough, I decide.

I call my sister, Aria, because I need someone to be at the house with Evie while I drive to the hospital. And I know she'll be up because she doesn't usually go to bed before 1AM. She's a decade younger than me, single and childless.

"A shooting? What do you mean?" she says.

"I don't know anything yet," I tell her.

"Okay, I'll be there in a few."

Aria lives a few blocks away, in one of the North End's few apartment buildings. It's purposeful, her closeness to me. I've always been like a mother to her.

I turn on the TV while I wait. There it is—breaking news on channel 7. The words across the bottom of the screen read DEADLY SHOOTING AT RAY'S BAR.

Deadly.

I taste bile in my throat.

The reporter on screen, a woman with frizzy hair and bags under her eyes, is standing in a parking lot, the sign for Ray's and police tape behind her, on the other side of the street.

"Details are still coming in, but we know there are at least three people dead," she says.

I turn off the TV, feeling like I'm going to vomit.

Then I see Aria pull into the driveway.